MARRIAGE SEASON

A PRIDE AND PREJUDICE VARIATION

ELEANOR HARDY

1

Summer 1810

"I cannot bear it any longer!" Kitty Bennet exclaimed, rising and pacing to the drawing room window. "If I remain inside for one more day I fear I shall go mad!"

"I suspect I already have," Lydia sighed, lying prone on the sofa. "It is so cruel of our father to keep us locked up like this."

Elizabeth Bennet had tried to be patient with her younger sisters but she had heard enough.

"You forget the cause of our incarceration, dear Lydia. Surely even you can agree that our father is acting in our best interests. Do you think he enjoys having us all here, arguing and bickering out of sheer boredom? He has forbidden us from leaving the house because he wishes to keep us all alive."

Kitty wrinkled her nose in disgust but she said nothing. How could she argue?

Nobody knew the cause of the influenza epidemic that was sweeping through parts of England. Some speculated that it had been helped by the uncharacteristically damp weather, but there had not been much chatter on the subject since many families had chosen to cloister themselves at home rather than risk infection. Not everyone in Meryton was so cautious, but the general agreement was that no balls should be held until the danger had passed.

Kitty shook her head forlornly. "I am willing to bet that the Lucas girls have been allowed to come and go as they please. I am sure I saw Charlotte and Maria walk past the other day."

Elizabeth sighed. She had to admit that she, too, was finding the extended isolation rather trying. She understood why her father had insisted upon it, though, and she tried to keep that in mind.

Mrs. Bennet had not taken her husband's decision at all well. She was wont to spend most of her time in Meryton, gossiping and plotting with her friends and sister. She had grumbled and groaned until the letter arrived from London to say her brother's daughter had fallen ill. She had not complained about their seclusion since then.

Her husband was rarely seen in those days. It often seemed as if he had permanently retreated to his library. Mrs. Bennet lamented what she believed must be his ill-health, but Elizabeth was well aware of the reasons for her father's withdrawal. He had scarcely been able to cope with his wife's hysterics at the best of times, but he had generally found some relief in the fact that she was often out of the house.

"I suppose it is rather wearying after all this time," Elizabeth owned, refusing to be further drawn on the topic.

That did not stop Lydia taking her modest agreement and shamelessly exaggerating it when their mother entered the room some time later.

"Mama!" Lydia cried, jumping to her feet. "Mama, even Lizzy is bored! Mary has not admitted it yet, but I can see that even she is feeling the ill-effects of our imprisonment."

"Hush, my dear," her mother hissed. "You must stop this. I fear my nerves will not be able to take much more! Why do you push me, girl? And you, Lizzy! You ought to know better!"

With that, she was gone from the room, though

they could hear her shrieking all the way down the hallway.

Elizabeth caught the eye of her elder sister Jane, who shot her a conciliatory look.

"I barely said a thing," she muttered.

"I know it," Jane agreed, shaking her head. "This quarantine is affecting us all rather badly. I do hope it ends soon."

Elizabeth sighed. It was difficult to know the extent of the problem. One could draw insights from the newspapers, of course, but she suspected they had been instructed to play down the severity of the outbreak. She knew it would have to end at some point, but it seemed like that end point was very far into the future.

"Mama is holding up quite well, all things considered," Jane whispered. "Imagine. It must be difficult enough to have five unmarried daughters in normal times when there are balls and parties to prepare for. She must be beside herself with worry now, with all of us out and not a ball to be seen for miles!"

"Yes," Elizabeth agreed, alarmed at hearing such a grave sentiment from Jane of all people. "But do not forget that everyone else is in the same situation as we are. Why, I imagine London is not a nice place to be at all, what with all of those people crammed into such a small area. It is lucky we were here at Longbourn when the outbreak began."

"Yes," Jane said wryly. "Though I have heard tales of some young ladies purposefully visiting grand old houses at the start of the outbreak on the off-chance that they might be urged to remain there by their concerned host. Can you imagine?"

Elizabeth laughed. "Keep your voice down. If mama heard you say such a thing... Well, all I can say is it is lucky that Netherfield remains unoccupied, because she would no doubt have sent us there on some errand with just such a scheme in mind!"

"Would that be such a bad thing?" Jane's eyes took on the faraway look that her sister had witnessed many times. "Can you imagine if some dashing young man had taken Netherfield and one of us happened to be visiting when father decided we must quarantine ourselves?"

Elizabeth could not help but roll her eyes. "Netherfield is indeed a fine house and the estate is the most beautiful in the area, but is it not a little fanciful to imagine a young gentleman taking it up? More likely, it would be an old man. And knowing our mother, she would dispatch not one but all of us in order to ensure that at least one of her daughters took his fancy."

Jane shivered. "Oh, Lizzy. You *are* wicked!"

They laughed then, because the prospect of anyone taking Netherfield was rather unlikely. The grand estate on the other side of Meryton had lain idle for many years, since the girls were children. Elizabeth could not recall seeing the previous occupant.

Still, the prospect of a newcomer in town and their mother's likely reaction kept them laughing long into the afternoon until dinner was called, and it was a welcome respite from the gloom that had settled over the house.

2

Mrs. Bennet's morose mood soon dampened the spirits of her older daughters as the family entered the dining room and took their usual places around the table.

"Oh, Mr. Bennet," she exclaimed, as her husband shuffled inside with a wary look on his face. "I am not sure if I can take much more of it. I told myself not to complain in light of my niece's condition, but I cannot hold back any longer. The girls are beside themselves with boredom and I cannot blame them. I fear they shall lose their girlish charms if this awful isolation does not end soon."

Lydia gasped. "Mama, how can you say such a thing? Father, it is unbearable! Am I to live the rest of my days as a spinster like my older sisters?"

Elizabeth glanced across the table and caught Jane's eye. Neither of them could hide their smiles, despite the cruelty of their sister's words. They might have been offended if anyone else had uttered them, but it was simply Lydia's way to think only of herself.

"I did not realise I had given up all hope of marriage."

Lydia glared at her. "Well, you may as well, Lizzy. You are getting on."

"My dear girl," Mr. Bennet said wearily. "You speak about this as if it was the end of society as we know it!"

"It may as well be!" Lydia cried. "I have not been out of this house for four weeks!"

"Would you prefer if we all journeyed to London and exposed ourselves to the sickness? You ought to know better after it nearly took your young cousin."

This silenced Lydia, though it did little for spirits at the table. They ate in silence, but it was impossible not to note Mr. Bennet's improving spirits as he sat at the top of the table in silence and ate his meal.

Finally, he sat back and chuckled. "Speaking of London. I received a letter from your uncle today."

"How are the children? Has little Madeline recovered? Oh, I do hope it was good news."

"Of course it was, Jane," Lydia said. "He would not smile if there was grave news, would he?"

"For once your sister is right, Jane. Now, if I may be allowed to finish," Thomas Bennet muttered, standing and pacing to the fireplace.

He was not at all sure what to make of the invitation he had received earlier that day. Edward Gardiner and his wife had been urged by their doctor to take young Madeline to the seaside as soon as was practicable. It was believed that the milder temperatures and the sea air would do wonders for the sickly child's health and aid her convalescence.

This, in itself, was unremarkable to Mr. Bennet. It was a common approach taken by those who could afford it. He had heard of similar suggestions on many occasions in his life.

No, what perplexed Mr. Bennet was the suggestion that the Bennets travel to Ramsgate to accompany the Gardiners.

He was still not sure what he wished to do. His was a comfortable estate, but it was still far more modest than many family seats. He expected some of his tenants would have trouble paying their rent in the coming months, thanks to the disruption caused by the influenza outbreak. Taking the entire family to the seaside in Kent would likely be a costly affair, though he saw some merit in it.

"Oh, Mr. Bennet!" his wife wailed, breaking his focus. "You must tell us what the letter said at once! I cannot bear it! I have not had any news from anyone in days now!"

She fell back in her chair so abruptly that his first impulse was to send a servant to fetch the smelling salts in case she had fainted. He soon saw that she had not; that she had simply worked herself up into such a state of anxiety that her face was red and her eyes watery. She had always been a spirited woman, but recent weeks had sent her almost wild with nerves.

He nodded to himself. That settled the matter. He could not take much more of being cooped up inside with his wife and silly daughters.

"Well, my dears, your uncle has invited us to join him and his family in Ramsgate. And I have decided to accept his invitation."

3

Longbourn House was a hive of activity for the remainder of the week and into the next week, as arrangements were made and trunks packed with gowns and sashes and anything else the girls could find to take with them. After all, Kent was widely reported to have escaped the worst of the influenza so it seemed likely that they would have far more freedom there than they had recently had at home.

Finally, the day of departure arrived. The whole household rose before dawn in order to make final checks and ensure everything necessary had been packed. Once this was confirmed, the footmen loaded the trunks onto the carriage, dismaying Mr. Bennet by suggesting that they might need another carriage for all of their belongings.

Thankfully that was not necessary, though they did need to unpack the carriage and begin again. It was a tight squeeze inside what with all the hat boxes.

"Can you not make do with the bonnets you're wearing?" Mr. Bennet groaned as he surveyed the cramped conditions in the carriage.

There was a chorus of objections, mainly from the younger girls. Elizabeth and Jane did not care if they could bring one bonnet or one hundred: they were simply delighted to be going to the seaside, especially when it meant they would see their beloved aunt, Mrs. Gardiner.

Mr. Bennet held firm and would not be bargained with. Soon they were departing, with a noticeably sullen Kitty and Lydia huddled together and looking as if they had been gravely wronged. Mr. Bennet winked at Elizabeth and she immediately understood his meaning and smiled back: he had not just only them more space, he had ensured that his silliest daughters would ignore him for most of the journey.

Elizabeth settled back against the cushioned seat and smiled. They were jolted this way and that by the movement of the carriage, but she did not mind a bit. She was simply delighted at the prospect of getting out and seeing something other than the walls of Longbourn House.

4

———

Fitzwilliam Darcy was restless. Derbyshire had not been badly hit by the influenza outbreak, but it had affected him nonetheless. His younger sister had been visiting their aunt in Kent with Mrs. Younge, her governess, when frenzied newspaper reports about fatalities in London began to appear.

His initial reaction had been to send for her immediately, but he had decided against it. He did not want to risk having her travel any way close to London and risk being exposed to the illness. Still, he was not entirely comfortable with how long the thing had dragged out: he had not expected it to last for so long.

"Dear, Mr. Darcy. You look rather sad. Come and join us for cards."

Darcy shook his head. "Not at all. You are mistaken."

That was the other way the outbreak had affected him. His dear friend Bingley had called on him at Pemberley with his sisters several weeks before. The Bingleys resided in London, which of course was the first place to be struck by the outbreak. He could not in good conscience allow his friend to return to London, so he had insisted the Bingleys remain on at Pemberley until the thing had been contained.

"Oh, I am not mistaken," Miss Bingley whispered, her lips forming a mischievous grin. "I am always right about these things."

"She is," her sister agreed. "Everyone says that about her. It's a gift."

"What?" Darcy muttered, despite his resolve not to engage with their nonsense. "Like one of those fortune tellers?"

This gave Miss Bingley great amusement. "Oh no, dear Mr. Darcy. Not at all. Why, those women are fishwives after a few bob. How can you compare me to them?"

Darcy said nothing.

"I know just the thing to improve your mood," she said, not dissuaded in the least by his silence.

"You must throw a ball! It would be a fine diversion for all of us."

"Caroline! We have imposed on Darcy's kindness quite enough without insisting he throw a ball in our honour."

"It would not be in our honour," she protested. "I suggested it simply as a way of cheering Mr. Darcy. He appears awfully glum, and I believe I have identified the reason. It is dear Georgiana, is it not? You must miss her so. Even so, she is probably having a capital time in Kent."

He nodded. "I am sure my aunt is simply delighted by her."

Darcy was saved any further invasions on his privacy by the arrival of his manservant with a letter. Darcy's spirits were greatly improved on seeing his sister's handwriting, though he did note that it was somewhat messier than her usual meticulous script.

He turned away as he opened the letter, wishing to savour its contents in private He was not disinclined to having company, but his present company seemed to always seek to *study* him; to understand his every move. Darcy found it remarkably tiresome, preferring as he did to simply go about his business in peace.

He smiled, unable to think an unkind thought when he had his dear sister in mind. He began to read, expecting to learn how she was getting along with their aunt and cousin. Lady Catherine was a formidable woman by all accounts, but Darcy did not doubt for a moment that she had been utterly charmed by Georgiana's goodness.

Darcy froze as his eyes skimmed over his sister's words and he realised that this was no routine dispatch about the goings on at Rosings.

"Oh my goodness," he muttered.

It was becoming very clear to Fitzwilliam Darcy that the contents of this letter must not be shared with anyone.

"What is it, Mr. Darcy?"

He turned and tried to force a smile. "Nothing at all. You must not worry, Miss Bingley. It does not concern you, but it is a matter I must see to at once. Excuse me."

He hurried from the room and waited until the door was closed behind him before he broke into a run.

5

"Ah, this is a tonic," Mrs. Bennet sighed as they strolled along the strand. "I fancy I might remove my shoes and walk along in the sea water. It is good for you, I hear."

Elizabeth smiled. There was so much to explore in the town that she was afraid she might miss out on something if she confined herself to the water's edge. "Perhaps I shall join you later. I would like to explore."

Jane linked her arm through Elizabeth's and leaned close to whisper in her ear.

"Is this not worth all those long weeks of confinement? Oh, Lizzy, it is so wonderful to be free again."

At this, Elizabeth could not help herself from

bursting into laughter. "Yes it is! I had not realised how much it had affected me."

"And me."

"Oh, Jane! You seemed in good spirits most of the time and even now. Mama is half mad from being cooped up and I could say the same for Lydia and Kitty! I do not know that a little bit of salty air can be enough to cure them!"

"Well I expect that this shall cheer them up: there is to be a ball on Saturday."

"A ball," Elizabeth repeated. It had been a long time since they had attended an assembly at Meryton, the closest town to Longbourn. "Why, perhaps Lydia was right to try and bring such a vast collection of bonnets! We must go and see what the milliner's in Ramsgate has to offer!"

"That's the spirit," Jane whispered, squeezing her arm. "Come. We shall leave mama to her bathing!"

ELIZABETH'S good spirits improved even more when they entered the milliner's shop. She was not usually the type of young woman to be driven wild by the prospect of a new sash or bonnet, but it was hard not to in this place. The little milliner's shop in Meryton was sufficient for their needs, but she would not hesitate to admit that its selection was rudimentary at best. Norbridge's Fine Millinery, on the other hand, was like a wonderland of colour and exotic materials.

"Oh my," Jane gasped. "Look, Lizzy! This headpiece is adorned with peacock feather!"

Elizabeth put down the rather plain but exquisitely-made bonnet she had been examining and moved to her sister's side. It was indeed a fine creation as Jane had remarked, and oh did the shop owner know it! The bonnet took pride of place in the shop, set on a smooth carved wooden head on a tall stand in the middle, which made it stand out from the others even more.

"Shall I try it on, Lizzy?"

Elizabeth laughed and shook her head. "I fancy, Jane, that this sort of thing might cost more than our father's yearly income! You had better hope that some young Earl or Duke takes it upon himself to attend the ball if you are serious about acquiring this one!"

Jane's cheeks flushed the most delicate pink. "Oh, Lizzy! I was just admiring it! You must think me greedy, but I assure you I am not. It does not matter to me if my bonnet is adorned with peacock feather or the most basic ribbon. Or nothing at all!"

"I know that, my darling," Elizabeth smiled, shaking her head. "I know you well enough to know that…"

She trailed off, leaving Jane watching her and waiting for her to finish her sentence.

"What is it, Lizzy? You look most perplexed. I told you—I was merely admiring it. I did not think for a moment that I might have the means to buy such an extravagant thing!"

Elizabeth shook her head, barely hearing her sister's words.

There were two young ladies standing at the back of the shop and they had, for some reason, captured her attention. She did not know why, which only served to puzzle her even more.

One of the ladies was much younger than the other. Elizabeth fancied she was of an age with Lydia; perhaps even younger. Even from a distance of several yards—which was what it must have been from the centre of the vast emporium to the back— it seemed that… Elizabeth shook her head. She did not know whether it was her imagination at play, but it seemed as if there was something furtive about the ladies' behaviour.

The young lady had a pleasant countenance. It was obvious that she was the shy sort—she seemed to defer to the other lady at all times, and she flushed violently practically every time her lips moved—which was not often.

The other lady was older: that much was obvious from a glance. She seemed bolder; more confident.

"Lizzy," Jane murmured. "What has happened? You have gone awfully quiet."

The older woman was foisting bonnets on the younger one, who seemed almost uncomfortable with the force of her ministrations.

Elizabeth shook her head and forced herself to look away. "It is nothing, my dear sister. I think, perhaps, it is another symptom of our recent confinement. I am now seeing suspicious things in the most innocent and routine behaviours.

"Whatever do you mean?" Jane asked, perplexed.

Elizabeth debated for a moment whether she ought to even disclose her strange fixation to her sister. It did not take her long: there had not been a matter yet that she had been able to keep from Jane.

"Those two young ladies back there," she murmured, conscious of being overheard and considered indiscreet. "It is… I do not know, dear Jane. As I say, I belicve our confinement has affected me more than I previously believed."

"What young ladies?"

"Exactly," Elizabeth said, taking Jane's confusion as confirmation that she had seen something odd in a perfectly normal situation. "I expect I would find them perfectly unremarkable if it were not for the fact that we have done little else but sit at home and read or work on our needlepoint."

Jane, surprisingly, did not seem comforted by this comment. In fact, her lovely face screwed up into an expression of the utmost puzzlement. "Who are you speaking of, my dear Lizzy?"

Elizabeth spun around, confused. She was sure the young ladies were perfectly ordinary, but even so, Jane ought to have been able to pick them out as the shop was not busy.

She frowned. The back of the shop was empty. "They were standing there a moment ago," she murmured.

There were a few customers dotted around the shop, but those were mainly older matrons, far older than the ladies she had seen.

"They were there," Lizzy added. She walked to the back of the shop, expecting to find that it had another entrance onto the street behind. It was, after all, quite a huge place.

There was no such second exit to the street.

"How very curious," Elizabeth said, pulling back a heavy velvet drape and seeing the staircase behind that most certainly did not lead out onto the street.

"Lizzy," Jane said, bustling after her and looking at her with a very serious expression. "Perhaps we had better return to the inn. I am worried about you."

Elizabeth shook her head. "You must not worry about me. I know what I saw."

"There was no one there, darling. If there had been, they would have been forced to walk past us in order to leave the shop. No one did so."

6

F itzwilliam Darcy did not waste a moment. He barked orders at his steward as he hurried from the house. The man suggested sending a boy ahead to instruct the stables to prepare his horse, but Darcy declined this offer. By the time the boy was sent, he would have reached the stables anyway.

This was no leisurely ride; this was a matter on which his very life depended. He had considered writing to his cousin to tell him the news, but he soon dismissed that thought. There was no time for letter-writing; not at a time like this. More importantly, Darcy was not sure he wanted to share what he had just learnt—not even with the colonel, despite the two men sharing a bond that made them closer than most brothers.

"Infernal idiot," he muttered to himself as the stables came within sight. He had trusted his aunt to care for his sister's welfare. He had even told himself that Georgiana might be better off in the care of a woman.

It now seemed that he had been mistaken.

Georgiana's letter had been brief, but it had still caused his legs to collapse from underneath him. The worst part of it was that he could almost picture her lovely face as if she had said those words to him in person. He could only imagine the girl's naïve delight at having encountered the man she thought was a faithful friend of her brother's.

"Scoundrel," Darcy snarled.

One of the younger stable boys jerked away in alarm. Darcy barely noticed.

No, Darcy's mind was squarely fixed on Ramsgate. He had never ridden there from Pemberley, but he had ridden to Rosings on one occasion. That had been for a lark; a bet to see how long it might take him. He had spent two nights at inns and not enjoyed a moment of it. There had seemed so little joy in the challenge that he had almost immediately regretted taking it up.

Now, there was more urgency and even less enjoyment to be had. He would ride all night and day if he had to. Even then he knew that he might be too late to stop them!

His mind raced as he tried to understand the circumstances that could have led her into Wickham's path. For one thing, it seemed to Darcy a very odd coincidence indeed. That she had left Rosings and gone to Ramsgate without his knowledge was odd in the extreme. What business did she have at Ramsgate, after all? He was sure he had been quite clear with her governess, Mrs. Younge, that any significant decisions as to her ward's care were to be directed to him in the first instance and to his cousin, the colonel, if Darcy could not be reached.

He had received no letter from Mrs. Younge.

And now Georgiana was in Ramsgate, and she had just confided in him that she had met George Wickham there and their intention was to marry! Not only that, but dear, faithful Georgiana had initially hoped to return to Pemberley at once and seek her brother's approval for the match. Her letter mentioned Mrs. Younge's assurances that Darcy would be overjoyed at the match and that they must not waste any time in settling the matter. After all, was Mr. Wickham not a handsome young man of style, and surely sought after by the most eligible young ladies in society?

On remembering this, Darcy kicked open the stable door.

"The cheek of the woman!" he cried, his face flushing violently as he recalled his sister's words. "The trickster! The fraud!"

There was nothing good about George Wickham, and anyone who claimed he was an eligible young man was either a liar or a fool or both!

Darcy's angry musings were presently interrupted by the hurried arrival of the stable master.

"My boy says he saw you hurry here, sir. Has something happened, sir? What do you need?"

"Jenkins," Darcy muttered, barely able to focus on the present. "Have my horse saddled."

"Which one, sir?" Jenkins laughed nervously and scratched under the flat cap that covered his balding pate. "You have fifteen of them."

"Oh yes, I suppose," Darcy muttered. He often talked at length with the man to select the most appropriate animal for the day's pursuits. Now, however, that all seemed rather fanciful. "Whichever one will get me to Kent in the shortest time."

"Kent?" the man repeated, slack-jawed. Seeing the determination on Darcy's face, though, he turned and hurried away, calling to one of his young apprentices as he did so.

Darcy stormed outside, his jaws working as he waited. Each passing minute felt like an hour. Time was palpable now; as it if was an hourglass with the sand rapidly flowing into the bottom vessel. When it was all gone, his sister's hopes would be gone with it.

He had worked so hard to protect her; to see to it that she had every advantage in life. Now it seemed that she had been cruelly tricked into throwing away any chance of happiness. And the worst thing was Darcy had not been there to protect her.

"Damnable fool!" he cried.

Jenkins emerged a moment later. He was leading a difficult stallion, the one they had named Lightning. Darcy did not usually pay much heed to the horses—he was not so sentimental as to name them himself. He generally relied on the suggestions of the grooms and stable master, being, as they were, more familiar with the animals than he was.

He remembered Lightning, though.

"This is the one we had such difficulty breaking in," he said.

"Right you are, sir. One of my boys took a few

falls from him. Stubborn, he is. But he's also stronger than the rest of them. He'll get you to Kent faster than anything. I can bring you one of the older stallions if you'd prefer one that's easier to handle."

"No," Darcy said, taking the reins. "Speed is of the utmost importance."

"You racing again, sir," Jenkins said with a grin.

"No."

"You're sure you wish to take him? He'll get you there fast but you know how difficult he can be."

"He will be fine."

Darcy hopped on the animal's back without another word.

"Where is your luggage, sir? Don't you want me to strap it on before you go? Shall I send a boy…?"

"That will not be necessary, Jenkins."

He had not thought to bring anything with him; nor was there time to prepare it. He took off, hurrying the horse as fast as he could go. There was no time to lose.

7

"Oh, Mr. Bennet," his wife cried as they sat down to dinner in the inn that evening. "Oh, it was a delight; it truly was. To bathe in that water. I feel like a new woman entirely."

"In spirit, perhaps," Thomas Bennet said wryly. He had opted not to join his wife and daughters on their walks. Instead, he had found an antiquated bookshop and had whiled away many hours in perfect silence, perusing the dusty volumes on offer there. He was as much restored as his wife claimed to be.

"Well I am and that's all there is to it. The water was a delight."

"I do not doubt it for a moment," he said. "Though I am sure you might have cause to reconsider when you catch a cold from being in there."

"Oh, you are a bad man!" Mrs. Bennet cried. "You'd deny a woman the only pleasure she has had in several months."

"Indeed," Mr. Bennet said, catching his second daughter's eye and smiling. "And how was your day, Lizzy dear? I take it you did not join your mother?"

She smiled. "I intended to but we became quite distracted by the shops in town. It is a charming place!"

"Oh the silly girls! We were not five hundred yards along the seafront when they disappeared off. Gone to look at bonnets they were! At the seaside! Honestly, we may as well have stayed at home and sent them off to Meryton!"

"We can return to Longbourn early if you like, my dear."

"Oh no!" his wife looked horrified. "It was an expression. I have no more wish to return to Long-bourn than I do to leap off a cliff."

Her father made some dry response to her mother—Elizabeth was dimly aware of the laughter in his tone. But she did not hear his words. She had looked around to see where Lydia had gotten to. She could not see her absent sister, but her eyes had landed on something far more interesting.

The two young ladies from earlier.

She turned back to Jane and tried to get her sister's attention, but it seemed Jane was distracted by a disturbance at a nearby table. She could hardly mention her daft notions aloud with the rest of her family present.

As it was, it had taken her the better part of an hour to convince her good-hearted sister that she had not taken ill; that she had been looking at two young ladies in the back of the shop. Jane had not believed her until she had reasoned that perhaps they were the shop owner's assistants, downstairs to display a new creation.

She had even started to believe this explanation herself, but now she knew better.

They sat at one of the tables at the back. And the younger of the two was certainly not a milliner's daughter.

Her dress was plain, but it was clear to Elizabeth that the material was expensive. Ramsgate may have been a step ahead of Meryton when it came to the fashion, but Elizabeth was confident that this dress had not come from Kent at all, but from one of the more exclusive dressmakers in London. Despite the young lady's awkward movements, it was still plain to see that the cut was exquisite; the tailoring perfect. No expense had been spared on this young lady.

Her companion appeared far less affluent, though the older woman had a far less modest type of dress than her young charge. Oh, she still appeared demure, but there was a sense of impropriety about her that puzzled Elizabeth.

"What are you staring at, Lizzy? I asked you a question."

Elizabeth turned to Jane, surprised to find her sister watching her.

"Over there," Elizabeth whispered, leaning closer to Jane so nobody else at their table could hear. "Do you see? The table in the corner. It is the two ladies I saw earlier."

Jane followed her gaze and watched them for a moment. There were plenty of people dotted around, so Elizabeth had not felt too awkward watching the women. Now, though, she began to worry that they might be discovered.

"Do not stare."

"I am not," Jane murmured, looking back at her. "Ah. You were mistaken when you said they were the shopkeeper's relations. They appear far too well-dressed for that."

"I thought the same thing."

If Elizabeth had hoped to hear Jane's theories on the matter, she was soon disappointed. Her sister began to reflect on what she might like to do the following day. Elizabeth found herself unable to concentrate.

She glanced back at the two women. Who were they? They appeared too close in age to be mother and daughter, and in any case, the elder's dress would surely have matched the younger's in finery if that were the case. Were they an affluent young lady and her governess? Elizabeth might have thought so if it had not been for the strange interaction she had witnessed in the milliner's.

What do I know of such things? After all, I have never had a governess, she thought.

But that was not the only odd thing she had noticed. The inn seemed a strange place for the two ladies. While it was a pleasant enough place and in no way insalubrious, Elizabeth was well aware that there were more highly-regarded inns in the town that seemed more appropriate for a young woman of means.

She frowned. Upon closer inspection, it appeared that the two women were now involved in some kind of disagreement. Elizabeth stared, wondering if it was her imagination making her see something suspicious where there was nothing out of the ordinary. But no, it was quite clear: the younger one looked on the verge of tears while her older companion appeared angry about something.

8

Amost fortuitous thing happened then. The Gardiners arrived down to dine. Upon approaching their relations' table, they asked the innkeeper if two chairs might not be brought over from another table so they might eat with their family.

The innkeeper was a rather ill-tempered man who appeared to make a sport of denying even the most reasonable requests. He scoffed, telling them his staff would do no such thing.

The Gardiners cheerfully accepted this, though Mrs. Bennet was affronted by the man's cheek. Her husband tried to calm her as the Gardiners walked across the crowded room to find another place to sit.

Elizabeth was aggrieved at first, but then she

saw something that interested her greatly. There must have been no other space in the place because the Gardiners took the table directly beside the two young ladies!

Before she could even question the wisdom of her intentions, Elizabeth stood.

"I must go and ask my aunt Gardiner where she found such a lovely ribbon for her bonnet."

And then, with a thumping heart, she set off across the room, guided by her strange fascination with the two women.

Elizabeth sat and greeted her relatives as if she had not seen them in days, though they had eaten together just that very morning. She pulled out a chair that backed onto the table when the two women sat and for a few pleasant moments, she chatted to her aunt and uncle about how they had spent their day. She was very much encouraged to hear that her young cousin's condition was already markedly improved.

They fell silent shortly thereafter when her aunt and uncle's food was brought, and this gave Elizabeth an opportunity to sit in silence and reflect on the day.

If she had thought that she would not be able to help overhearing the conversation at the adjacent table, she would have been wrong. In fact, the two women spoke in such hushed tones that Elizabeth really had to strain to hear them. She was immensely glad that she sat with her back facing them because it required a great deal of concentration to hear their whispers.

One of them—Elizabeth believed it must have been the older one—had a deeper voice and a worldlier accent. The other lady had a hesitant air about her—it could only belong to the nervous young lady she had now encountered twice that day.

"Are you sure, Mrs. Younge," the quieter said. "After all, I would not wish to upset my darling brother."

"You will not upset him," the other snapped, though her voice was as low as her companion's. "I told you."

Why, Elizabeth wondered, *do they feel such need for secrecy? All around us there are large and boisterous groups. None of those people have tried to lower their voice in the slightest. Why, I could shout at the top of my voice and even still only those at the tables closest to me could hear me with all this noise.*

"All the same, I... I... oh, it does not feel right

to me. I am sure he would love to be there to see me married."

"Yes, but you must act quickly. He is a very eligible young man, your Mr. Wickham. And he is uncommonly fond of you."

The quieter girl laughed: it was clear that she was both flattered and embarrassed by this. "Oh I doubt that. Why should he be? I am no great beauty."

Elizabeth could not help but be struck by her modesty. The young lady she had seen, though nervous and still rather girlish, had been unmistakably handsome.

"All the more reason to marry him as quickly as possible," the other one said with an unmistakable urgency in her tone. "You don't want to lose him, do you?"

"No," the young lady said, her voice rising. "No, of course not! I love him!"

"Hush," her companion scolded. "What did I say about keeping your voice down? The walls have ears in places like this."

"But why the need for such secrecy? We are doing nothing wrong, like you said."

Why indeed, Elizabeth wondered. *Why, indeed.* It was clear to her that they were discussing a marriage. None of her sisters had married, but that did not mean she knew nothing of the ceremony. She was a young lady, after all, and she had spent countless hours with Jane discussing all the details of such occasions, right down to the minutiae. She also had friends who had married, so she was not entirely ignorant of such things.

It struck her now that this seemed a very odd way for a chaperone to behave. There was no breathless excitement on the part of the young woman. If anything, she seemed fearful. And far from addressing her concerns and comforting her, it seemed to Elizabeth as if the older woman was attempting to force the girl to act irresponsibly.

I must stop this, she said to herself. *I am not some heroine from the pages of a novel. This is real life. And real life is far more mundane than those exciting tales would have one believe. It is probably nothing more than a case of nerves. She seems the type.*

Elizabeth resumed her conversation with her aunt, who had by now finishing eating the inn's hearty stew. Still, though, the two ladies played on her mind even as she and Mrs. Gardiner discussed their plans for the next day.

And an opportunity soon arose that allowed her to discover a little more about the mysterious pair.

9

"Blast it!" Fitzwilliam Darcy cursed at the top of his voice. His determination to ride through the night had not weakened a jot, but his horse appeared not to share the same enthusiasm. "I should have known a young fellow like this would not relish the prospect of going on in the dark."

And it was dark. It had been an unpleasant, drizzly sort of evening and the cloud had not let up at all as evening turned to night. It was impossibly dark.

It struck Darcy that his stable master had not anticipated his desire to go on through the night and he himself had been far too agitated to think of laying out his plan in any detail. Now he was stuck: there simply was not time to turn back and change horses. It was out of the question.

They continued on at a far slower pace than Darcy might have liked.

"I suppose, old chap," he muttered to thc horse. "It is better to proceed slowly than to have an accident in the dark."

He shivered at the thought. He had not informed the colonel of his plans. If he were to be incapacitated in any way, there would be no one to stop Georgiana from marrying. Indeed, if he was gravely injured and Wickham proceeded unimpeded, that unpleasant young man would find himself the master of Pemberley.

It was so unthinkable that Darcy shuddered with displeasure at the thought of his father's beloved estate falling into the hands of a young man who had falsely represented himself to the older Darcy.

"I will not allow it!" he roared into the clammy night air.

HE WAS FORCED to reconsider his plan in the next town. He had no idea where he was, but it did not matter. The road was particularly bad in this area, and there had been a few occasions where horse and rider had very nearly met their end on the uneven surface.

The emotional nature of recent events had rendered him even more fatigued than he might usually have been. In fact, he was sure that even if it were bright, he would have had difficulty seeing straight.

So it was with that in mind that he came to a stop at the first inn he encountered.

It seemed a most unwelcoming place, but Darcy did not care at all. Despite his disappointment at having to stop, he had managed to come a long way. It was possible that he might make it to Ramsgate the following night if he set out early enough.

He took a room and refused the innkeeper's offer of stale bread and ale, that evening's meal having long since been served to the last late diners. Mercifully, he was asleep almost as soon as he retired to his Spartan quarters, though his dreams were monopolised by the man he feared might soon be his brother by law.

10

E lizabeth Bennet was reluctant at first. Thanks to a lull in the conversation at her table, she heard the younger lady behind her announce her intention to retire for the evening. She might have ignored it completely were it not for the other's response.

A couple of things struck her.

Firstly, she was still ignorant as to the identity of the younger lady, though she had long since learnt that the older was a Mrs. Younge. Was she imagining it? She tried to think of her conversations with Charlotte and her other friends. Did they not frequently use her name, usually in amusement at some odd statement she had come out with?

The oddest thing, though, she thought as she watched the shy young thing walk past, was the almost brusque way in which the other woman had accepted this. There was an almost hostile tone to her voice, as if she had reached her very last shred of patience.

It is very odd indeed, Lizzy thought.

She watched the young lady depart. She seemed so very unsure of herself and Elizabeth felt a pang of sympathy for her. How strange it must be to stay in a place like this if one was shy. The place was positively bursting with people, all of whom were strangers. Even Elizabeth felt the place was a little intimidating, and she had many relatives present! And to think that the girl's companion had not seen this and sought to ease her discomfort!

Elizabeth stood before she quite knew what she was doing.

"Are you retiring?"

She nodded. "Yes, I think I shall. I am rather tired."

"Very well," Mrs. Gardiner said with a smile.

"Oh, come on now. I thought we would all play at cards. What do you say?"

"Lizzy is tired, Edward! You must let the girl go."

But her uncle would not be dissuaded. "It is still early yet! We shall play just one game. Come on;

before the others join us and the arguments break out over who ought to play with whom and such."

He was smiling at her so kindly that Elizabeth found she could not resist. She sat down, telling herself it was for the best. After all, if she chased after the young woman to ask after her welfare, she would probably only succeed in frightening the poor young lady half to death.

ELIZABETH WAS QUITE ENJOYING their game once they got started. She had not turned around to look at Mrs. Younge, but had assumed that young lady must have retired for the night.

So she was mildly surprised when, some time after her young companion left, Mrs. Younge spoke. She was greeting someone. Elizabeth had been so focused on her cards that she had not seen anyone approach. She was on the verge of spinning around to see who had joined the woman, but she managed to stop herself in time. It did not pay to show one's curiosity quite so blatantly.

"Yes." The young man's greeting was strange for its total lack of enthusiasm or warmth.

Perhaps he is her husband, Elizabeth thought,

suddenly intrigued by the set-up again. *And they have grown rather weary of one another.*

"Yes? That's all I get? You'd be thanking me if you knew what I'd had to put up with." Her voice was coarser now than it had been, and the difference was not a subtle one.

"Keep your voice down. And I don't know what you're complaining about. It's not as if you're doing this out of the goodness of your heart!"

"George! What a thing to say! You think it was an easy matter?"

"Easiest money you've ever I'd say."

The young man sounded well-educated, but he was certainly not a gentleman, Lizzy thought, more intrigued now than she been in a long while. It was not just that, though. She felt a strange feeling in her chest; certain that this somehow affected the young lady with the light hair and sweet voice. It was odd: Elizabeth did not know the girl at all, yet she felt a strange kind of protectiveness towards her.

"Your turn, Lizzy!" Edward Gardiner said, frowning at her. "My goodness, girl. You are exhausted. I must apologise. I assumed you wished to hurry off upstairs to read or write letters to your young friends back in Hertfordshire. I did not think you were actually exhausted."

She smiled and shook her head. "Do not worry. Yes, perhaps the sea air has tired me."

"Is it all set?" Mrs. Younge was asking behind her. "I don't think I can take another day of this. And there's always the brother to think of. He is so very protective—it is maddening."

"As I well know," the man called George said. "I grew up with him, remember? He is insufferable."

"Well, she wants to tell him. Imagine! He'd put a stop to the whole thing!"

"She won't tell him. Not if you've done what you were supposed to."

"Of course I did," she said, sounding annoyed.

"Well you better have. The last thing we want is him getting wind of it and trying to stop the wedding."

"That's why I asked if it's all sorted, my dear. We need to get you two to Scotland as soon as possible. I told you: their aunt is the nosy sort. She looked down on me so! I don't doubt that she shall have her writing things out already, complaining to Darcy about our sudden departure!"

"Stop worrying! We shall leave tomorrow. We'll be in Gretna by the end of the week and married as soon as we possibly can be. Then Darcy won't be able to do a thing about it. He'll just have to accept me as his brother and hand control of her fortune over to me as its rightful master!"

"George! You mustn't say such things; not here!"

"Oh, look around," he said, his voice getting louder. "I chose this place for a reason. Do you think anyone around here knows the family? Darcy would never condescend to associate with anyone who'd stay in a place like this."

Elizabeth's eyes widened. For a moment, she forgot her compassion for the young lady and reflected that this Darcy fellow must be a terrible sort if he was capable of showing such prejudice.

"Well you never know," Mrs. Younge was saying. "Can't be too careful. I've risked everything for this. I'm not going to lose it because you wish to be careless."

"Relax. Come on. We'll have a drink."

She sighed. "I cannot. She probably already thinks it's odd that I have not joined her. I simply could not bear it. She goes on so; so worried about what her dear brother thinks. She has no mind of her own."

Elizabeth had heard enough. Every instinct told

her to leap to her feet and do something before it was too late, but she worried that the time to do so had come and gone. After all, this Mrs. Younge appeared to be about to retire upstairs for the night and who knew what early hour they would depart at!

"Just one," the man said, sounding merry. "You deserve it for a job well done. And it might make your young charge more tolerable!"

Elizabeth was on her feet within seconds. "I am sorry," she said, sounding as weary and uninteresting as she could. "But I am struggling to keep my eyes open. Perhaps Jane could join you for the rest of the game?"

She did not wait to hear their response before she hurried off.

11

"The young lady; the one with the light hair who was sitting over there behind us… can you tell me what room she is staying in?"

The innkeeper narrowed his eyes and glared at Elizabeth Bennet as if she had just asked him to carry out a most inconvenient favour for her benefit.

"What do I look like? A post master?"

"No," Elizabeth said as pleasantly as she could with her heart hammering the way it was. "But she is a friend of mine. I forgot to ask her what room she's in. So silly of me. I have a book for her."

"How sweet of you," he snapped. "And I have an inn to run."

"Please. I'd hate to go knocking on all the doors upstairs and disturb your other guests."

"You'll do nothing of the sort," he snapped.

"I'm afraid…"

"Fine! She's in the room at the end of the hall. Don't you go causing a disturbance now with your giggling and your foolishness. We have people here who want to sleep."

"I shan't." She hurried off before any of her party saw her speaking to the man and came to see what the problem was.

———

ELIZABETH HESITATED before knocking on the door, but urgency made her reconsider her hesitation. She had no idea how long it would take Mrs. Younge and her friend to drink their gin, and she did not wish for them to know about her visit to the woman's young charge. She knocked on the door as gently as she could, wary of frightening the young lady.

The door opened and a pale face looked out. "Oh. I thought you were Mrs. Younge."

"Hello," Elizabeth said, somewhat lost for words. It was a unique situation—one she had never found herself in before.

Elizabeth thought she saw a glimmer of fear in

the girl's eyes. She swallowed. "Look, may I speak to you for a moment? I know this is strange, but it's rather urgent. We can ask the maid to remain with us if it would make you feel better."

The young lady appraised her before standing aside to let her in. "No it's quite alright. I am not afraid of you. I am Georgiana Darcy."

Elizabeth realised she hadn't even thought to introduce herself. "I'm sorry," she laughed. "How rude of me. Elizabeth Bennet."

"I'm pleased to make your acquaintance even if it is rather…"

"Odd. Yes I know. Look, I know this may come across as rather impertinent, but I overheard something that I felt I ought to…" she stopped and shook her head. "You must forgive me. I could not help overhearing part of your conversation. You mentioned your brother and I gather you are to marry soon."

Georgiana flushed a violent pink that seemed impossible for someone with a complexion as pale as hers. "Yes," she said after a prolonged pause.

"It seems…" Elizabeth fought to think of a delicate way to put it, but there seemed to be none. "I am so very sorry to intrude on you like this. You must forgive me. I simply… well, it seemed to me that you were distressed about the whole thing in a way; that you were being convinced not to tell your brother."

"He is rather strict," she whispered, before flushing again. "Not in a bad sense, of course. He is my brother. He is wonderfully kind and generous. He is my guardian, you see."

Elizabeth nodded. "And Mrs. Younge?"

"My governess."

"Ah." Elizabeth swallowed. Part of her wanted to hurry away and hide after making such a fuss. To call her behaviour impertinent would be an understatement. Yet, she could not stop herself! To hear those two talking downstairs had been to glimpse a different world of greed and cruelty.

"Well, you see not long after you left she was joined by a young man. George is his name, I believe."

It was impossible to miss the transformation that happened in the young woman on hearing that man's name. Her eyes lit up; her smile widened. It was quite clear that she had significant feelings for him. Elizabeth could not help but smile at the sight of her—though her smile soon faded when she remembered his callous words.

"He is to be your husband?"

"Yes," Georgiana whispered, her smile still lighting up her whole face.

Elizabeth was now faced with a dilemma. She had heard half a story, if even that. Oh, she had her suspicions as to the nature of this George fellow. But it was also clear to her that Georgiana—who seemed a remarkably pleasant young lady—loved him. To tell her what she had overheard would surely cause the young lady grave injury.

"What is it, Miss Bennet? Has something happened to him?"

12

There was not a sound in the room apart from that of the fire crackling in the grate. Elizabeth Bennet stared at her new friend, wishing she knew how to approach this matter with grace and tact.

If she was wrong, she risked causing the young lady no end of heartbreak. But what if she had assessed the situation correctly?

Well, it had sounded to her like Mrs. Younge and the young man were in cahoots; as if Mrs. Younge was not the kindly chaperone who had helped Georgiana to plot her elopement, but something else entirely.

Her mind worked to fill in the gaps in her knowledge. They had talked about a fortune and it was clear from Miss Darcy's attire that she was wealthy. What honourable young man would attempt to lure an heiress to Scotland to wed in secret rather than pursue her hand openly?

Unless the brother did not approve…

But I do not know this brother, she thought. *Perhaps he is a tyrant. I fear if I act now, I may end up making things worse for this delightful young lady.*

"What is it?" Georgiana asked, having grown quite alarmed now. "Please tell me nothing bad has happened to him!"

"No," Elizabeth said, moving to her new friend's side. "No, nothing has happened to him. I simply… well, look. I suppose I overheard your conversation and I became a little concerned. It appears your companion is very eager to see you married without your brother's knowledge."

Georgiana smiled. This time it was more guarded. "Yes, I suppose. She is older than me and more worldly. My brother is my guardian, as I have said, so it is very difficult for me to go behind his back."

"Why would she wish for you to do that?"

"Oh, you know. I am young and naïve and I do not see things as they are. She is worried that he will move on and find some other young lady if I do not marry him soon." She flushed the same shade of violent pink as she had earlier. "He is very hand-some, after all."

Elizabeth had not seen the man—she had only heard his voice. But now that she reflected on it, he did have the self-assured tone of a gentleman who had never had to worry about attracting female admirers.

"That may be so," she said, choosing her words very carefully. "But you are beautiful and he would be a fool to seek another bride simply because he is too impatient."

Georgiana shook her head. "You are too kind."

"I speak only the truth," Elizabeth said firmly. "Besides, it would not be very honourable of him to act in such a way, would it?"

"I suppose not. But Mrs. Younge says I am young and idealistic. That I must face reality. Oh, Miss Bennet, I know it sounds foolish, but I love him so!"

"Then," Elizabeth laughed. "Send an express to your brother and seek his permission. Wait a few weeks and marry your love without all the secrecy!"

"I suppose," Georgiana said, not sounding at all convinced. "In any case, I have written to my brother to tell him. Mrs. Younge told me not to but I could not help it. He is so good to me, you see."

Elizabeth was somewhat heartened by this.

"What will he do, do you think?"

"Oh I expect he will not be at all happy," Georgiana said, looking fearful. "He will be frightfully disappointed. But what can I do? I love George! I have known him since I was nothing more than a child and he has always been so kind!"

"He is a relation of yours then? Or the son of the nearby estate?"

"Oh goodness no! He is the son of our father's steward. He grew up with my brother."

"So he is not a man of means."

Georgiana looked saddened by this. "That is why Mrs. Younge says we must hasten to Scotland at the earliest opportunity. She thinks my brother will run him out of England rather than allow him to marry me. Fitzwilliam is very proud, you see. And protective."

Elizabeth looked around. They had been sitting there for several minutes and she felt that Mrs. Younge might burst in at any moment to return to her room. She had no idea what to do. It crossed her mind to hurry downstairs and seek the counsel of her aunt Gardiner, but she had no way of doing that that was guaranteed not to alert Mrs. Younge. All it took was one misplaced glance or word from her aunt and the other woman might become suspicious. She already struck Elizabeth as the cautious sort.

"Perhaps your brother can be persuaded."

"George does not think so," she said, shaking her head sadly.

"Well, what do you wish to do? You have told me what Mrs. Younge wants and what your darling George wants. What do *you* want?"

Georgiana smiled shyly. "It would make me very happy to have dear Fitzwilliam walk me up the aisle in the chapel at Pemberley, not at some blacksmith's forge in a town where I know nobody." She whispered those words, but there was a definite force of feeling behind them.

"Well then," Elizabeth said. "That is what you must do."

"Ah, but it is not so simple. Mrs. Younge is adamant that I must act fast or risk losing him."

"That is hardly the case. A young man's love—a good young man's love—is not so fickle." Elizabeth knew little about love that she had not read in the sort of novels her father despised, but she carried on in earnest. It seemed like the most important thing in the world to her now to prevent this young woman from entering into a disadvantageous marriage, and to do so in a way that would not reveal to her the cruel manipulations and false declarations she had fallen victim to.

"He is a good man."

"Well then," Elizabeth urged. "He will wait for long enough to get your brother's blessing."

Georgiana Darcy was not convinced. "I am afraid," she whispered, now close to tears. "What if…"

Elizabeth saw to her dismay that she did not have a chance of changing Miss Darcy's mind. The conspirators had done too good a job at convincing her speed was of the essence.

Another thought struck her just as she was starting to give up hope.

"I have a plan," she said, trying to hold back her excitement. "I think I have a way of delaying matters without seeming to do so."

"Whatever do you mean?" Miss Darcy asked, frowning.

13

I t was almost ten the following night by the time Darcy arrived at the inn his sister had mentioned in her letter. Apart from a few loutish men, the ground floor of the inn was quiet. Darcy shook his head. He could not stand the thought of his dear, sweet sister staying in such a place, though when he reflected upon it, the alternative was far more troubling.

"My sister," he said to the innkeeper. "I believe she is staying here and I must speak to her immediately."

"At this hour, sir? Why didn't you come a little earlier?"

"I left Derbyshire the day before yesterday," Darcy snarled. "Believe me. I came as quickly as I could."

"Good lord," the man said, momentarily stunned in the face of such a journey. "What did you say her name was?"

"Miss Darcy. Miss Georgiana Darcy."

"She must have left," the man said, after perusing the ledger in front of him. "I see no Miss Darcy here."

"What?" Darcy hissed. "When did she depart?"

The man flicked a few pages and grunted. "She didn't."

Darcy had little patience for such a vague answer. "Do not test me, man. Either she is here or she is not!"

"She was never here!" the man protested. "You can see for yourself!"

Darcy frowned. This was highly irregular. He pulled out the letter he had received, crumpled now from being in his pocket for the whole journey. "It is here. Is this not the Cutler's Arms."

"The very same."

"Well then…" he thought of something. "What of a Mrs. Younge? When did she depart?"

The man flicked through his book. "She didn't, sir," he said after a pause. "She's still here. And there's a young lady with her by the name of Miss

White. Always thought she was a bit well-to-do looking for keeping that sort of company." He looked up at Darcy. "No offence."

Darcy didn't have time to take offence. He lurched towards the stairs before the man even had a chance to direct him to his sister's room. He paused and looked back and the man barked directions at him. Darcy raced up the stairs.

—————

Mrs. Younge opened the door with a smile on her face. It soon vanished when she realised who had been knocking.

He pushed against the door and entered the room without bothering to greet her.

"Where is she?"

"Mr. Darcy! Such a pleasure to see you! She's not—"

"Where is she?" he asked, glowering at her. He had had about all he could bear of this place. He simply wanted to get out of there with his sister and take her back to the safety of Pemberley.

"She's not…"

He could not stand it anymore. There were two

doors leading off the little sitting room they were standing in. He burst through the first one and looked around. The bed was neatly made—it was clearly unoccupied. Groaning, he turned and marched to the other room. It, too, was empty, though the bed sheets were twisted and untidy.

"You see?" Mrs. Younge said plaintively. "Why would I lie to you, Mr. Darcy? You are my employer after all. And a good one too."

"Rather a fool, as it happens," he muttered, despising the woman. "Where is she? You must tell me now before I lose patience."

"That is what I have been trying to do, Mr. Darcy," she said, giving him the sort of patient smile he might have expected from a kindly aunt, not the scheming woman who had helped to plan his sister's downfall.

"Go on then. Sometime before midnight if you please."

"Oh, Mr. Darcy! You are…" Her smile faded as she saw he was not reacting kindly to her attempts at being charming. "Oh, it is no good. She is in with the other young lady. It was quite impertinent, you see. Miss Darcy was taken ill rather suddenly, and that young lady rather insisted that she be taken to their quarters and cared for there! Barely seen her, I have!"

"What young lady?" Darcy snapped, barely able to keep his patience. "Where is she?"

"Oh, I shall show you. I am glad you're here, Mr. Darcy. The impertinence of them!"

14

Elizabeth paced around the little anteroom off the room she had previously been sharing with Jane.

"It is most irregular, Lizzy," said her aunt, the only one who knew about their secret guest apart from Jane.

Elizabeth had kept it a secret all day, fending off the increasingly demanding requests from Mrs. Younge to visit her charge. For Georgiana's part, she had acted so convincingly listless that Mrs. Younge's resolve to leave Ramsgate had diminished somewhat. She had insisted, rather half-heartedly, that there was no need for the Bennet girls to take care of Miss Darcy; that that was her duty. Elizabeth did not trust her not to pack the poor girl into a carriage bound for Scotland regardless of her supposed sickness.

"I know that, aunt," Elizabeth said, shaking her head. "And I am sorry I kept it from you today. I felt I must tell one of you. Will you please keep it from my parents for the time being? Mama would take it up all wrong and then we would lose any hope of discretion. And papa... well, I don't know that he would care as such, but perhaps..."

"Lizzy," Mrs. Gardiner said, putting her hand on her niece's shoulders and smiling affectionately at her. "You must not worry. By all accounts, you are doing this young lady a great service. I hope she appreciates that."

"Well I hope she shall never know! It is my intention to stop her from knowing the callous way the young man spoke of her. And she believes he loves her! It is tragic. All I can hope for is to delay the scheme until the brother arrives. And if he is a good guardian to her, he must surely see the danger she is in."

"Indeed," Mrs. Gardiner said. "Now, I must go and check on the children and retire myself. Do you need anything?" She frowned. "Oh, Lizzy. I know you mean well and you have the kindest heart I have ever known, but are you sure you want to get involved in someone else's affairs? We are only here for a matter of days. What happens when we leave?"

"I do not know," Elizabeth said with a sigh. "I felt I had to act, but I must admit I don't know how I can protect her if... well, it all depends on her brother. She said she had written to him and confessed the whole folly. With any luck—if he has any sense—he shall come to find her and take her back to safety. But they are from Derbyshire so I do not know if he could even get to Ramsgate before—"

"Derbyshire!" Mrs. Gardiner cried at a volume Elizabeth feared might wake their sleeping guest in the next room. "Why Lizzy, you must know that I spend my younger years there. Where, pray tell, did she say she hailed from? I wonder if it was anywhere near to Lambton, where I am from."

Elizabeth frowned. Young Miss Darcy had mentioned a place, but it had seemed insignificant at the time. It was only when she recalled the conversation between Mrs. Younge and George that she recalled them naming the place as well.

"Pemberley, I believe. I haven't the faintest idea where that—"

"Pemberley!" Mrs. Gardiner cried, even more

frenzied than before. "What did you say her name was? Not Darcy; surely not!"

Elizabeth nodded mutely. For the sake of discretion, she had not mentioned any names to her aunt. "Yes. How did you guess?"

"My dear," Mrs. Gardiner said, looking shaken. "It is a matter of… You see, Pemberley is one of the finest estates in Derbyshire! It is the home of the Darcys—has been for centuries. Oh, my dear. What have you gotten into?"

ELIZABETH WONDERED the same thing as she sat on the sofa. Jane had gone off to pile into bed with Mary; much to the latter's disgust, no doubt. Elizabeth had thought of doing the same, but she was suspicious enough of Mrs. Younge's motives to linger behind. She made herself as comfortable as she could on the little sofa in the anteroom with the thin blankets Mrs. Gardiner had found for her.

What have I gotten myself into? she thought.

It heartened her somewhat that Mrs. Gardiner was aware of the Darcys, not that she knew either of them personally. Elizabeth's final thought before she drifted off to sleep was that she might prevail on her aunt to write to this Mr. Darcy and urge him to make haste to Ramsgate if he did not already plan to do so.

She smiled, feeling a weight lift off her mind. Because she knew she could not hold off Mrs. Younge and her friend for very long. They were too determined for that.

———

ELIZABETH SAT UP WITH A START. She knew immediately what had woken her: someone was still banging on the door. At first she thought it was morning and she had accidentally slept too late, but she soon saw it was dark outside. Pitch dark: not even close to dawn.

She got to her feet, back aching from lying on the rather uncomfortable sofa. She knew who it was and she was beginning to lose patience with the woman. She was glad of the chain on the door: she intended to use it.

"I told you," she said, pulling the door open and not even bothering to confirm her suspicions. "She needs to rest."

Her eyes widened when she saw who it was. Well, she did not recognise the furious-looking gentleman outside the door, but she could say for certain it was not Mrs. Younge.

"I do not know who you are, sir," she said in a loud voice. "But you must—"

Next thing she knew, the door was flying open and he was storming into the room looking very agitated indeed. The chain hung uselessly from the door, no match for his strength.

"I don't know what you think you're doing!" she cried. "But this is my room. How dare you come in here and—"

"Where is she?"

"You look here now! I heard you talking down-stairs. I know the truth. And I won't allow you to…"

"Take me to her at once!"

She paused and blinked, looking at him more closely. Nothing about this man—not his fine clothing or the imperious tone of his voice— seemed to match her memory of the fellow from the inn. She gasped.

"You're Mr. Darcy, aren't you? Georgiana's brother?"

He seemed taken aback. "Yes. Of course," he snapped. "Who else would I be?"

15

He stared at this woman. He was barely able to see from tiredness, but there was something about her that caused him to take a second glance all the same.

A moment later, he chided himself for his folly. Was that not the way of women like Mrs. Younge? He realised that now. They charmed and cajoled until you were blind to the very danger of them. He ought to have seen it coming. His inaction had risked…

Had risked? It was not over yet. He cleared his throat and stared at the woman sternly.

"Take me to my sister at once. I will accept no more of this treachery."

She stared at him, unblinking. He thought he

saw defiance in her eyes, but it was gone a moment later. She crossed the room to the door.

"Where are you going? I ordered you to take me to my sister. Did you not understand?"

She pushed the door closed and turned back to face him. This time, there was no doubting the ice in her eyes.

The gall of her, Darcy thought. *To trick my sister into coming here and then have the cheek to blame me for showing up to take her to safety!*

"I thought it best," she said coldly. "To close the door and not allow our neighbours to see you in such a state of rage."

"State of rage?" he blustered. He was dimly aware that it was a wise idea; something he had not thought of, but he was too consumed with anger to consider it further. "Of course I am angry. Now, take me to my sister at once or the consequences for you shall be even graver!"

"She is sleeping," the woman said, her eyes like chips of ice, though Darcy had to acknowledge that they were very fine eyes indeed. "As was I. It is late after all. Should you not take a room here and you may then—"

"I will do no such thing! I did not ride all the

way from Pemberley to lay my head in a disreputable establishment such as this!"

She shook her head. "What a strain it must be."

Darcy had had quite enough of this from Mrs. Younge's aide. In fact, he scarcely knew why he had listened to her for so long instead of summoning the innkeeper and having him round up all the villains.

"I shall ask you one more time. Where is my sister?"

The woman turned her back on him, seemingly offended by his behaviour. He could not think why —after all, it was his family who had been injured by these scheming scoundrels. "She is in there," she said, pointing at a door on the far side of the tiny, stuffy room.

He glanced around as he hurried to it, seeing the blankets on the sofa. "Ah, so you are her guard." He wrinkled his nose, appalled to think of his poor sister being kept under lock and key.

"I did not do this for appreciation or to earn your thanks," the woman said, sounding offended. "But I must say I might have expected a little more from you than such blatant hostility."

Darcy shook his head as he rapped on the door and called his sister's name. This woman's conduct was appalling. But he had more important matters on his mind.

His heart soared with happiness when he heard the soft, familiar voice from the other side of the door. He reminded himself that it was too early to be relieved: he still had not yet ascertained what these scoundrels had done to his beloved Georgiana.

16

Elizabeth Bennet stood by the now-cold grate and watched the man. His posture was proud and uncompromising, and it seemed to her that his character could be described in the same fashion.

She was equal parts galled and amused. Her only wish was that she had persuaded Jane to remain on the sofa with her, for how was she to relay the events to anyone who had not witnessed the man's utter hostility?

This Mr. Darcy, she was sure, was the most pompous, arrogant man who had ever lived!

She had meant what she said. She had not intervened to take Miss Darcy away from those people in order to ingratiate herself with the Darcys. After all, she had never even heard of them before that point.

It was clear to her that Mr. Darcy thought differently. She had seen the way he looked at her and she felt sure she understood the hostility in those dark, serious eyes.

He believed she had helped his sister for financial gain. He thought she was no better than Mrs. Younge and her friend George, willing to go to any lengths in order to extort money from the wealthy classes.

I am a gentleman's daughter, she thought, glaring at him as he opened the door and went inside. *Yet you treat me with all of the hostility and distrust that you might show to a common criminal!*

Miss Darcy appeared at the door, her eyes bleary and half-closed from sleep. "Fitzwilliam! Oh, my dear brother, what a pleasure it is to see you after such a long time!"

He greeted her just as warmly, though there was an unmistakable urgency in his tone.

"Ah," Miss Darcy said, coming into the little room that was barely more than the size of the boot room at Pemberley. "I see you have met Miss Elizabeth Bennet. She has been ever so kind to me. We met yes—"

"I'm sure she has been remarkably kind," Darcy

snapped. It was clear from his tone that he believed no such thing.

Elizabeth shook her head, unable to believe the man's conduct. Had it not been for his sister's presence, she might have rebuked him for addressing her in such a way. As it was, she felt such protectiveness over the young lady that she said nothing—but only out of respect for Miss Darcy's feelings.

"She has," Miss Darcy said, clearly not hearing the nuance in her brother's tone.

Darcy shook his head. "Where is the servant? I shall have her gather your things at once and forward them once I have secured our lodgings."

"But it is the middle of the night, brother! Can we not just stay here?"

He glowered at Elizabeth. "That is out of the question."

"I shall prepare at once," Miss Darcy said, returning to Elizabeth's room and closing the door behind her.

Elizabeth had no desire whatsoever to speak to the brother, but she felt obliged to tell him of the treacherous plot she had overheard in the inn the night before and the modified version of the story she had told his sister in order to save her feelings.

Swallowing her dislike of the man, she crossed the room and stood before him.

"I must speak to you now that we are alone," she murmured, careful to keep her voice low. "I need to tell you the truth of the matter, which you may not have been apprised of."

His lip curled. "I see."

"I am afraid you do not. You see, I encountered Mrs. Younge and—"

"No." He held his hand inches from her face. "I will listen to no more lies and deceit from you people. I have heard quite enough."

"But Mr. Darcy," Elizabeth gasped. "I know not who you refer to when you say 'you people', but I can assure you—"

"You are all the same! I will not hear it! I am no fool, and I will not be subjected to further machinations on the part of… of…"

He was now red-faced with indignation. Elizabeth gave the appearance of being calm, but beneath the surface was a different matter. She had never been so insulted in all her life and she could scarcely believe what she was hearing.

"Save your words, Mr. Darcy," she said, turning and walking to the door. "I shall leave you in peace as you wait for your sister and spare you the pain of having to spend time in the company of 'you people', whatever that is supposed to mean."

She marched out without waiting to hear his response: she had been insulted quite enough for one evening. She doubted that man could open his mouth without uttering something cruel and disparaging.

17

"Come along, Georgiana. I wish to leave this place immediately."

A few moments later, his sister opened the door. "I am ready." She looked around the room. "Where is Miss Bennet? I cannot leave without thanking her."

"Thanking her?" Darcy asked, outraged. Then he took a breath and made himself smile.

It was typical of his kind-hearted sister to see the best in people. He imagined that was how they had tricked her into travelling here. Of course it made sense that she looked on that young woman favourably. They had probably been nothing but nice to her as they manipulated her into doing what they wanted her to do. His suspicion was confirmed by her next statement.

"And," she whispered, not meeting his eyes. "We must tell dear George that we have moved. Otherwise how should he find us?"

Darcy shook his head. "My dear sister. I cannot allow you to marry him. It is out of the question."

"But why?"

He was not a sensitive man, but even he was touched by the sight of her large, frightened eyes. He could not fail to see the pain in them. How was he to proceed? He had been her guardian for years now, but this was beyond his expertise. That was the reason why he had engaged the services of Mrs. Younge: a young lady needed an older woman in her life.

Not that that had ended at all well.

"You must trust my judgement."

"But I love him," she pleaded, still unable to look at him.

Darcy's heart sank. Even though she spoke those words softly, he could not mistake the determination in them. He did not doubt her for a moment.

What was to be done? He would sooner let his sister grow old alone than he would allow her to marry a cad like Wickham. Wickham would have been the ruin of her; he had no doubt about it.

But it was late and she was tired. He shook his head. "For now, let us remove ourselves from this place. I shall find us more suitable accommodations and we can talk in the morning after we have slept."

Her mood improved immediately and he could tell she had misinterpreted him. Still, he had not the heart to disappoint her: it could wait.

A plan began to form in his mind. He would see his sister to a more suitable inn. Then he would return and find Wickham. He would pay the man whatever it took to make him leave. After all, was it not a small price to pay for his sister's future and happiness?

"Are you sure we cannot find Miss Bennet before we depart?"

"Yes," he said, trying not to sound exasperated. "It is late. I am sure she is sleeping."

"Very well. But I must see her tomorrow. She was so very kind to me; she insisted on taking me here and coming up with a plan to give me more time so I could wait for your arrival. I like her very much."

If Darcy's opinion might have been swayed by his sister's words, the likelihood of that happening was diminished by the fact that he did not hear a word of what she said. He had walked on ahead, scanning the corridor for a maid who might be dispatched to pack his sister's belongings and deliver them to the next inn forthwith.

18

I t would have to do, Darcy thought. The second inn was scarcely better than the one in which he had found his sister, but it had one benefit: George Wickham and his associates were not in residence. He waited until Georgiana was comfortable before sending for two maids and instructing them to remain outside his sister's door until he returned. He would have felt more comfortable had his own servants been in attendance, but he had, of course, not thought to bring any on his hurried dash to Ramsgate.

Georgiana and Mrs. Younge had travelled with a maid, but he was not confident that the girl was not under the control of the scheming governess.

He hurried downstairs and roused the innkeeper again, offering to pay him handsomely if the man acted as sentry and refused to allow anyone entry into the inn until Darcy returned. He was a genial man who readily agreed once he sighted the shillings that Darcy proffered.

He hurried through the dark streets, trying to calm himself. He knew George Wickham well enough to know that there was no sense in losing one's temper with the man. Wickham would only use it to his own advantage.

No, he knew how Wickham worked. The only way to get through to him was by appealing to his mercenary nature.

"You again," the gruff old innkeeper said. Darcy shielded his eyes from the lamplight. He had grown accustomed to the darkness on his walk there.

He did not bother to respond. He hurried upstairs and rapped on the door of Mrs. Younge's room.

There was no response.

He twisted the doorknob and was surprised to find the door unlocked. When he entered, he soon realised why. The room which had previously been strewn with her things was now empty. The bed was still a mess but it was clear that the occupant had vanished into the night.

He hurried out, heading straight for the room where he had found his sister. That room, too, was empty.

Darcy groaned. So all of the scoundrels had vanished into the night. He did not delude himself that they had gone far: he knew Wickham. He knew that man would not give up so easily—not when there was so much money at stake.

He resigned himself to spending the rest of the night hunting through the less salubrious establishments of Ramsgate in the vain hope that Wickham was foolish enough to be seen in such places when he knew Darcy was looking for him. He knew well that it was unlikely.

19

"Lizzy, are you sure you are well?" Mrs. Gardiner whispered as they walked along the seafront after breakfast.

"I am worried about her, aunt," Jane agreed. "I cannot imagine being accosted in such a way! I would have fainted!"

"I have told you both," Elizabeth said resolutely. "I am perfectly fine. Now, I told you what happened because it was odd. I did not tell you so that you could fuss over me. Yes, the gentleman was shockingly rude and prideful, but I can only thank the heavens that I shall never have to encounter him again. The only thing I feel is pity for his sister, who is a dear girl. That such a shy and gentle creature could have as a brother such a domineering fellow… well, it simply beggars belief."

Mrs. Gardiner shook her head. "Well I know I said it before, but it bears repeating. He ought to have thanked you from the bottom of his heart instead of accusing you of being out for his money. What a way to go on!"

"Indeed, aunt. I cannot imagine the man is very happy at all if he goes about seeing the very worst in people. I was only trying to help his sister. I must say, though, perhaps we ought not to judge him too harshly. After all, he must have been out of his mind with worry about his dear sister. I believe he said he had ridden directly from Pemberley and barely stopped."

"Never mind, my dear," Mrs. Gardiner said, taking her arm. "I expect there will be a great many kind and agreeable young gentlemen at the ball this evening. They will more than make up for Mr. Darcy being unsuitable."

"Unsuitable?" Elizabeth could not help but laugh at the understatement. "Why, that is the very least of it! You do not think, surely, that I looked upon him in any sort of favourable way after the way he greeted me?"

When their aunt did not respond, both Elizabeth and Jane stopped and looked at her. Mrs. Gardiner shook her head.

"I am sorry, my dears. I did not mean to offend you. It is just that his fortune is so great that I suppose it is hard for me to believe the young gentleman is anything but eligible."

"Trust me, aunt," Elizabeth said, shaking her head at the memory of her encounter with Mr. Fitzwilliam Darcy. "There is nothing eligible about him. Why, I would not give him a second glance if he was first in line to the throne!"

She looked up and was startled by what she saw. There ahead of them, approaching them at a remarkable pace, was none other than Mr. Darcy.

"There he is," she muttered to her relations. "Now you shall see for yourself that there is nothing appealing about him. He is the most loathsome gentleman I think I have ever encountered!"

20

Fitzwilliam Darcy had had a fruitless morning. His search the night before turned up nothing, just as he had suspected it would. He could say a lot of things about George Wickham, but he could not claim the man was stupid. Wickham may have turned down his offer to pay for his education, but that was not for want of intelligence. Wickham possessed an alarming level of cunning, the likes of which Darcy had never seen before.

Not only would he need to think carefully in his dealings with Wickham, he would have to work hard to find the man at all!

He had spent hours walking the streets the previous night, visiting establishments that should never have played host to a gentleman of his standing. He had been to the lowest gambling dens and drinking houses; places that he would never have imagined entering.

And yet he had. He had walked among the wretched and had found no sign of Wickham. Yet he was certain the man was close at hand.

Darcy had resumed his search early that morning, returning to the inn only to partake of a light breakfast with his sister. Sleep had made Georgiana even more hopeful that her marriage to Wickham might garner her brother's blessing.

Darcy was more aware than ever that time was of the essence. It was unfortunate that he was running out of places to look for his friend-turned-foe.

He came to a fork in the street and looked both ways, trying to decide on the best route to take. His eyes landed on the seafront and an idea formed in his head. Had not Georgiana's letter mentioned how she had been surprised to meet Mr. Wickham as she strolled along the water's edge with her untrustworthy companion? Perhaps that was the rendezvous point that had been arranged between them.

He hurried along, wondering if Wickham was waiting somewhere on the sand. It was turning into a fine day, and already crowds of visitors were making their way towards the water with their shoes and stockings off. This, of course, was the great draw of Ramsgate, and he suspected it was busier than ever after the influenza outbreak that had ravaged a large part of the country.

He rushed down the steps and looked around. There was no sign of him, but there were too many people about to be able to tell for sure if he was down there. He hurried along, growing increasingly frustrated. There was no sign of Wickham and the man was not exactly inconspicuous.

He had almost reached the other end of the strand and was about to give up when he saw her.

He had only encountered her for a matter of moments the day before, yet he recognised her immediately. There was something proud and attractive about her walk. She was with two others that he did not recognise.

Are they co-conspirators? he wondered, his temperature starting to rise.

Without another thought, he hurried forward. She would tell him where Wickham was hiding and he would resolve this ugly business once and for all.

When he was within twenty yards of the little group, he saw to this alarm that the young woman was watching him. His first thought was that she would naturally try to run off and evade his questioning. He walked faster, looking around to see her likely route so that he could track her movements if he lost sight of her.

Then he noticed something curious. She made no attempt to escape. In fact, she continued walking towards him as if she was not one bit frightened!

She does not care! he thought, very much alarmed. Perhaps Wickham has met his match in this co-conspirator. *A worrying thought indeed.*

He was almost level with them now.

"You there," he commanded when he was close enough that he did not need to shout.

She reacted in the most astonishing way. Instead of trying to flee, as he might have expected such a character to do, she carried on walking towards him, turning her head to each of her companions in turn and smiling—actually smiling—as if somehow this were all a joke to her.

Darcy was aghast. "You find this amusing?"

She stopped a few feet short of her and stared into his eyes without shame or embarrassment. "Rather amusing, yes. I see sleep has not improved your manners, Mr. Darcy. What a pity that is."

He watched her, rendered almost dumbstruck by her reaction. "Where is Wickham?"

She shook her head. "I do not know the man. But if your treatment of him is anything like your treatment of me, then I hope for his sake he is long gone from here."

"Answer my question," he growled. "I am well aware that you are lying and I will not tolerate it."

"Lizzy." The older woman stepped forward and took the arm of the young woman who had guarded his sister on behalf of George Wickham. The woman looked at him. "I do not know you, sir, but I'll thank you not to speak to my niece in such a derogatory fashion. She has done nothing wrong. In fact, she only sought to help your sister."

"No doubt that is what she has told you. You must urge her to tell me the truth of it—that is, if you are a decent woman yourself."

The woman baulked. "Do you make a habit of such conduct? I must say, having been reared in Lambton I might have expected better of the son of Mr. Darcy. I never had the pleasure of meeting him, but he was well-regarded in those parts."

Anger coursed through Darcy. "So that is your game, is it? You knew who I was and you saw fit to ingratiate yourself to my poor impressionable sister in the hopes that she might have a favourable word to say about you."

"That is not it at all!" the younger woman with the fine eyes exclaimed, stepping forward and squeezing the arm of the one who professed to be her aunt. "Please, sir! You have insulted me quite enough! I will not stand for more and I will not hesitate to go and find my father and uncle and notify them of your conduct. In the meantime, please wish your sister the best from me. God alone knows how she came to be such a pleasant, well-mannered girl with you as her guardian!"

Darcy was about to reply, but she spun on her heels before he could do so. He watched in disbelief as she stormed off, flanked by her aunt and the other young lady who bore a passing resemblance to her.

For the first time, he felt a stirring of misgiving. He could not explain it—had he not seen with his own eyes that she was involved? Yet she did not seem the type. He was left with the unshakeable feeling that this woman was a woman of honour despite her criminal connections.

He did not reflect upon it for very long, however. He had more pressing matters at hand, for if he did not find Wickham and banish him soon, he would have to shield his sister from that man for the rest of their days.

21

"Oh, Lizzy. Oh, I am sorry. I knew I should have told your father. It is unacceptable behaviour for a man of his station."

"You must not tell my father," Elizabeth whispered.

She had been shaken by this latest encounter with the awful Mr. Darcy, though she did not wish to dwell on it. How could he have judged her so harshly when she had the best of intentions?

"I fear matters have escalated far past the point where I ought to have told Thomas," Mrs. Gardiner muttered as they made their way across the strand and up the steps to the street that would lead them to their inn. "I could only do so much to protect you and in that respect I failed. Why, Edward would be appalled if someone had the audacity to address one of our girls in such a manner."

"He is upset," Elizabeth said as calmly as she could. "I know it is unacceptable, but I believe he is seeking someone on whom to release his anger."

Her voice was calm and her words sounded reasonable to her ears, but inside she was anything but calm. She would never admit it to anyone, but her heart stung with the harshness of Mr. Darcy's words. Was that how he viewed her? As a lowly beggar willing to act like a kind friend in order to have a few pennies thrown at her by a grateful brother? It beggared belief!

She had not expected anything from him. She had been relieved to see him at her door once she realised that he was the girl's brother and not the scheming young man who wished to marry her. Well, as far as he was concerned, it seemed she was no better than those who had sought to trap Miss Darcy in a disadvantageous marriage!

"Lizzy?" Jane's face was etched with worry. "Lizzy, you are awfully quiet."

"Jane, I am just reflecting. You must not worry. Please. Both of you must promise me you will not tell my father. It would only upset him."

"He needs to know," her aunt said, sounding like her mind was made up.

"Yes, Lizzy. Come on, now. Let us return and tell father. Then we can go and find ourselves new sashes for the ball tonight."

"I do not think, Jane, that the ball is such a good idea."

Lizzy baulked. "No, aunt. You cannot punish Jane for my sins. She did not know what I planned. It was I who urged her to go and sleep with our sisters so I could offer Miss Darcy sanctuary in our room."

Mrs. Gardiner shook her head. She looked horrified. "Oh my dearest Lizzy! I am not seeking to punish either of you! All I want to do is protect you. And I am quite decided on it. It is not safe for you to be here; not when there are angry young gentlemen stalking the streets and accusing you of all sorts. No, I think it is best if you leave Ramsgate.

"Oh, do not look at me like that. Look here. Edward and I have spoken at length about making a journey north to the Lake District. I would be delighted if you would join us when we find the time to travel. Would you consider it? I know it is not much of an immediate consolation. I would invite you to stay in Gracechurch Street for a time, but I believe you are more at risk of falling ill there than you are at Longbourn."

The offer made Elizabeth feel somewhat better, but she was still feeling deflated by the time they walked in the door of the inn. She could not stop thinking about his words; couldn't shake the image of his face, etched with anger. He truly had insulted her more than anyone else had ever done so. The truth was she wanted to be as far away from that man as possible. She did not care if she never set eyes upon him again. And why should she? He had a vast estate in Derbyshire. No doubt he would consider her part of Hertfordshire too inferior to ever even contemplate setting foot there.

22

By late afternoon, Darcy was beginning to feel light-headed. He had not eaten since breakfast, yet he was not inclined to rest until he had completed his mission. It was only when he almost toppled over onto an apple cart that he saw the error of his ways.

He entered the nearest inn without regard for its shabby exterior.

The broth was basic but hearty. Of course, it was nowhere near as fine as the food he was accustomed to, but what did it matter? He was so hungry that that cheap broth tasted finer than some of the best meals he had ever been served.

He had just about finished and was mopping his bowl with the chunk of thick country bread when he happened to glance up in the direction of the staircase.

He was on his feet immediately, though George Wickham had seen him at about the same time as he had noticed Wickham, so he had turned and fled.

Darcy caught up to him when he was fiddling with the lock of a door at the end of the first floor corridor. The sour smell of spirits was overpowering.

"Look at you," Darcy said with disgust, pulling the keys from his hand and opening the door. He marched inside, pulling Wickham with him.

Inside, the source of Wickham's intoxication became clear. There was a bottle by the bedside, the remaining half-inch of amber liquid giving a clue as to what it had once contained.

"Fitzwilliam Darcy," Wickham leered. "High and mighty as always. It's good to see you haven't changed a jot."

Darcy was about to respond with his fists, but he soon regained control of his temper. There was no sense in lowering himself to Wickham's level. Nor was there any sense in trying to convince Wickham to see the error of his ways. He knew now that there was no hope of redeeming the man. He was lost; perhaps he always had been.

"Indeed. Well, we do not have much time."

A FULL HOUR LATER, Darcy emerged from the inn, immediately brushing off his overcoat in an unconscious attempt to brush off the filth of the place. It had taken quite some time to get through to the man. How did one get through to someone like that?

Darcy sighed. Wickham's vices had long been a source of pain and disappointment for him, but he had to admit he was grateful to one in particular at that moment. Greed. Oh, Wickham had spoken at length about how unfair Darcy was being; about how old Mr. Darcy had had great regard for Wickham. Darcy had let him go on, not bothering to correct his former friend that his situation was entirely of his own making.

After all, Darcy had been fully intent on fulfilling his father's wishes and giving Wickham the living of the rectory attached to Pemberley. He would have had more than he ever needed, but he had refused to join the clergy. There was no point in mentioning this, Darcy knew. No good would come of it.

No, he was a couple of hundred pounds poorer now, but at least he had gotten rid of the threat that was George Wickham. He knew better than to give that man all of the money and expect him to keep his promise. No, he would speak to a solicitor at his earliest convenience and arrange for a stipend to be paid subject to Wickham adhering to certain conditions. Most importantly, that he stay away from Pemberley and its occupants for the rest of his days.

Viewed like that, Darcy thought, *it was a rather good deal indeed.*

23

D arcy's sense of satisfaction soon disappeared when he returned to the inn and realised that he still faced the task of telling his sister there would be no wedding.

With his mind and pockets full of money, Wickham had offered to write her a letter—for a price, of course. Darcy had dismissed his wretched offer, reasoning that he ought to tell her himself.

He owed her that much.

"There you are," Georgiana smiled, bowing her head when he entered the room. "What have you been doing? If it pleases you I would very much like to go for a walk and take some air. It is so stuffy here."

"Of course it is," he said. "I asked the maids to

keep the fire as warm as possible so that your cold does not return."

"My cold? Oh, Fitzwilliam! I told you. That was all a ruse. I tried to tell you."

"Tried to tell me? Georgiana, dear, you must not fib. There is no shame in being ill but you must take care to keep yourself warm when you do. You know this."

"Of course I do," she laughed. As much as he liked to see her in such good spirits, it filled him with sadness that he would soon have to ruin her good mood by announcing their imminent departure for Pemberley.

"Well then. There will be no walking until you are recovered."

"I was not ill, dear brother! It was an idea Miss Bennet came up with. She was worried about me. Remember? I tried to tell you but you were so worked up that you probably did not hear me."

"No," he said. "No, I do not recall. Anyway, I am glad to hear you are well. We shall depart for Pemberley at first light tomorrow."

Her face fell, just as he had expected it was. There was no chore quite as bad as delivering upsetting news to his dear sister. He sat down heavily in the chair opposite her.

"Look, my dear. I cannot allow this marriage. I have my reasons. You must trust me—that is all I ask. I do not believe George Wickham is a good enough husband for you."

She buried her head in her hands. "But I love him. Do you understand?"

"Yes," he said, meeting her red-rimmed eyes. "I am afraid I do. What worries me is his... my dear; he is not an honourable man. I cannot go into details but I will not have you marry him. Even the manner of his asking for your hand—it was sneaky. A true gentleman would have come to me and asked my permission, not arranged for you to sneak away and meet in secret. Do you understand? I suppose I cannot expect you to. You are young still."

She wiped away her tears with the handkerchief he handed her. To his surprise, she nodded. "I do understand," she said quietly. "I didn't at first, but Miss Bennet explained it to me."

"Miss Bennet," he said, frowning. "Who is Miss Bennet? I do not think I have made her acquaintance."

A tiny smile momentarily broke through her miserable expression, like the sun peeking through a gap in the clouds. "You have! I have mentioned her several times now. And she was with me that night you arrived! You were very unkind to her."

"Only because she had conspired with Wickham to help him marry you in secret. You can see why I was angry. It was all very underhand indeed."

"No," Georgiana said with surprising force. "No, that wasn't it at all. She does not even know George." Her voice faltered when she said his name.

"Perhaps that is what she led you to believe…"

"No, Fitzwilliam. You have it all wrong. She came to me a few nights ago. She had overheard my conversation with Mrs. Younge. You see, I was hesitant to marry without your blessing and I told Mrs. Younge so. Well, Miss Elizabeth heard this and she grew concerned for my welfare. She came and knocked on my door and we had the most extraordinary talk. She is ever so nice. She told me I must not feel pressured to marry. Mrs. Younge was worried that George would find somebody else if I did not marry him at the earliest possible time, you see. Well, Miss Elizabeth told me that was nonsense; that I must follow my instincts and wait if I must. And if George were to leave me because I would not marry him in secret, well so be it. That made him a dishonourable man I would not wish to marry at all.

"She said all this and I listened. She was so pleasant but I still... oh, I did not want to disappoint either of them. She could see it. So she came up with a scheme. I told her I had written to you, you see. So she decided I ought to take to my bed and pretend to be unwell. That was a way of delaying the matter until you arrived, see? I was hesitant but she rather insisted."

"I see," Darcy said, feeling very confused indeed.

"Yes," his sister said with her usual earnestness. "You see? That is why I wished to find her and thank her."

"You wish to thank her?" he echoed. "I do not understand. You wrote to tell me of your desire to marry Wickham. Now it seems this woman has prevented you from doing so. Why do you wish to thank her?"

"Because," Georgiana said. "It happened as she said it might. Oh, I told her all about you as we chatted that day. We did little else. She brought me to her rooms so that I could be free for a while, for she could tell that Mrs. Younge's insistence was difficult for me to bear. I told her how good you were for taking care of me; how fond I am of you.

"And at some stage in the afternoon, she turned to me and said 'maybe, Miss Darcy, if your brother objects to the marriage, he has a reason for it that you are not aware of'.

"Well, I did not accept it at first. The two of you are like brothers, after all. But then she helped me to see. You only want the best for me, so if you do not want me to marry George then perhaps I ought not to marry him. Oh, I love him so and my heart is in pain, but I can see the *sense* in your decision and I accept it."

He stared at her, a thousand questions bursting to be asked at once. How could he have gotten the situation so gravely wrong? He had injured that brave, wise young woman so gravely by his assumption that she was working with Wickham. Well, it seemed now that she was the sole reason that his sister's good name and fortune had been preserved.

He stood, uncharacteristically anguished. "Where is she? When I went to find her and Mrs. Younge at the inn they had both vanished."

His sister frowned. "Perhaps she was out. I know she is here until tomorrow with her family.

They are attending a ball tonight. She told me her sisters are very excited about the prospect."

"Well then there is not a moment to lose," he said, hurrying to the door.

"Wait," Georgiana exclaimed. "May I accompany you? I wish to see her before we depart."

"I shall bring her back here with me when I find her," Darcy muttered, rushing out the door.

If she will even deign to see me after the lousy way in which I addressed her, he thought miserably as he raced down the stairs.

24

"Here he is again," the innkeeper said, looking up from his ale. "Rushing about here as if he owns the place."

Darcy barely paused. "I must see her. Miss Bennet. The young lady who cared for my sister."

"Too late," the man said.

Darcy coloured, thinking the man was referring to Darcy's treatment of her. Had everyone in the town heard? Come to think of it, he didn't much care: all he cared was clearing up the matter with that young lady. He hurried towards the stairs.

"Didn't you hear what I said?" the man called after him. Darcy was moving so fast that the words didn't reach him.

He got to the top of the stairs and rushed forward, banging on the door to the room where he had first seen her. At first he thought she must have gotten wind of his arrival and she was refusing to open the door, but then it opened a crack.

"Who is it? What do you want?" It was a man's gruff voice.

Darcy took a breath. He was not accustomed to acting in such an indecorous manner but it was important that he put things right. "I need to speak to your daughter, sir. It is a matter of some importance. You may have heard."

The door swung open. Darcy noticed the chain had not been fixed; further evidence of his unreasonable behaviour.

"My daughter?" the man said.

"Yes," Darcy said, as patiently as he could. "Please. It is nothing untoward, I assure you. She was involved in a matter with my sister and I owe her an apology."

The man looked at him as if he was half-mad, but he turned and yelled something incomprehensible all the same.

Darcy waited, wondering what he might possibly say to her that would atone for his frightful behaviour. A moment later, a child rushed to the door, hair wrapped up in ribbons.

"There."

"What?"

"My daughter."

Darcy stared at the man. "No. I mean your daughter. Your adult daughter. She must be twenty or thereabouts."

The man shook his head. "This is the only one I've got."

Darcy turned without another word. Had Georgiana been mistaken? He walked slowly down the stairs as he pondered his next move.

───

"Tried to tell you, didn't I?"

Darcy understood now. "They've gone?"

"Slow on the uptake, aren't you? I suppose that's common enough in your sort."

"Well where have they gone? I was under the impression that they didn't leave until tomorrow."

"They were supposed to. Came back here this afternoon they did, the young ladies. Hurried off as soon as the gentlemen returned. Something must have happened." The man grinned. "You know how it is. I expect one of them has had her heart broken by a young gentleman who promised her the world and turned out not to have a shilling to his name!"

No, Darcy thought as he turned away. *No, a brave, kind young woman has been treated in the cruellest way by a man who should have known better.*

He saw it all again as he walked back to the inn. She had tried to tell him she was helping Georgiana but he had jumped to conclusions without even listening. He had been cold and abrupt when really he owed her a debt of gratitude that was so large it was practically unquantifiable.

He knew nothing about the woman, save that she had been willing to help a young lady in need. He walked along with his head bowed, which was unfortunate for him: if he had paid more attention, he might have recognised the woman up ahead as the aunt of the young lady he had offended so grievously.

Had he done so, he would no doubt have applied to her for more information about her niece and begged her to pass on a message of his most sincere regret at the misunderstanding that had caused him to offend her so profoundly.

As it was, Darcy kept his head down, deep in thought. He was reflecting on everything his sister had said. He concluded that perhaps Georgiana had learned more about the woman than just her name.

As he passed the Gardiners, Mrs. Gardiner elbowed her husband rather sharply in the ribs.

"Edward," she hissed. For once she did not care if she was overheard, but Darcy appeared so entranced that she doubted he would hear. *Probably consumed by his own importance!* she thought. She was not a spiteful woman, but she was still aggrieved at the frightful way the man had spoken to one of her favourite nieces.

"What is it, my dear?"

She turned back and watched Darcy go. "That's him! That is the awful fellow who spoke so cruelly to Lizzy this morning."

Edward Gardiner squinted after him. "Do you think I ought to go and have a word with him? It is no way for a gentleman to behave."

"No," his wife sighed. "I simply do not think it would do any good. He is a bad sort. There will be no changing him, that's for sure."

25

October 1811

M ore than a year had passed since the family's visit to Ramsgate.

Elizabeth busied herself with reading and walking and enjoying the renewed social life in Meryton after the influenza outbreak was widely deemed to be over. Her thoughts occasionally returned to her encounter with Mr. Darcy in Ramsgate, but she never reflected on it for very long. After all, they had no acquaintances in common and she thought it very likely that she might not ever set eyes on him again. She still thought fondly of his sister and hoped that that young lady had been able to find any sort of happiness in what Elizabeth felt must have been a very straitened life at Pemberley.

A rumour went around that a young gentleman by the name of Mr. Bingley had taken up the lease on Netherfield House. This only served to make Mrs. Bennet even more frantically obsessed with her daughters' marriage prospects. After much goading, her husband had been prevailed on to visit the young man, and an acquaintanceship had been formed, much to Mrs. Bennet's delight.

After all, it put her in an advantageous position compared to that of the other mothers in the area.

"Quick, Lizzy, attend to your hair," she urged as her daughters prepared for the assembly that was to be held at Meryton that very evening.

Elizabeth laughed at her mother's panic. "But mama, I thought it was Jane you wished to match with Bingley. It is all you have talked about for days now!"

"Oh, shush you! You shall drive me to despair with your insolence, I am sure of it! No, do you not recall what I said? Mr. Bingley has gone to London for the sole purpose of gathering his party for the assembly! Here! At Meryton!"

At this, Elizabeth could not help but smile. She had to admit, privately, that it was an exciting prospect indeed to think of several eligible gentlemen descending on Meryton.

"Very well," she said, hurrying up the stairs. "I shall drape myself in finery and make you proud."

"Oh that you would!" her mother cried.

"MAMA IS QUITE BESIDE HERSELF," Elizabeth laughed as she came into the room she shared with Jane and closed the door.

"That makes two of us," Jane said, struggling to tie the ribbon on her bonnet.

"Oh there now. Why are you so worked up? I am sure he is perfectly pleasant."

"No doubt."

"Well, then. There is no need to worry."

"What if he does not like me? What then? Mama has her hopes up so much that I am afraid of disappointing her."

"Oh, Jane," Elizabeth said, unable to believe her sister's inability to see her own beauty. "I don't see how he could fail to like you. You are nothing short of lovely."

Her sister flushed.

"It is the truth! Now I must prepare myself.

Mama says Bingley shall have quite the crowd with him and I am to do all I can to make myself agreeable!"

THE ANTICIPATION in the assembly room had soared to astonishing levels. All of the locals were in attendance and had been there practically from the moment the doors were opened. All were eager to catch a glimpse of the newcomer to their midst. Of course, rumours had spread about the five thousand a year he had in income, which had only stoked the flames of their curiosity.

At last he entered the room. Elizabeth looked to her sister, hoping that Jane would not be disappointed by the events of the evening. She feared it would not be the case, and she was soon proven right when Bingley's eyes landed on Jane and appeared to become stuck on her.

Elizabeth smiled to herself and looked past him to the rest of his party. Directly behind him were two young ladies, who must have been his sisters. They were followed by two gentlemen, one a rather indolent-looking chap. The other was tall and...

Elizabeth froze in horror. She grabbed at the

glass that had slipped from her hand. She caught it in time, but that said more about her agility than it did about the state of her nerves at that moment.

It was him! It was the awful Mr. Darcy, the one she had told herself she would never have to see again.

And when she looked up he was staring straight at her!

26

D arcy was in no mood for a ball, but his friend Bingley had rather insisted. He went along, ever the dutiful friend. He did not see the sense in attending. It was a small, dreary-seeming town—at least that was the impression he had formed as they raced by in the carriage.

Looking around now, he saw that his fears had been confirmed. Every woman in the place eyed Charles Bingley as if he were some sort of game to be hunted. Darcy had no doubt that they had heard of his friend's income and almost immediately set about pushing their daughters on him.

Darcy sighed inwardly as they made their way into the room. He looked around, getting a feel for the place. It was certainly nothing like the great ballrooms he had visited in his time. This was...

He baulked, a cry escaping his lips which he swiftly masked as a cough.

Miss Bingley turned and looked at him. "Are you alright, Mr. Darcy?"

"Yes of course," he muttered.

But he was far from it.

He had questioned his sister at length about the young woman who had rescued her from Mrs. Younge's clutches. To his dismay, Georgiana was able to talk at length about how wonderful and generous her new friend was, but she had been unable to provide any useful facts which might have allowed him to trace the woman.

He had learned, for example, that she had travelled with her parents and four sisters. But Georgiana had not been able to tell him where they had travelled *from*. Likewise, he knew she had relations in London, but he did not know their names. For all he knew, they could have been neighbours of his, but what was he to do? Hurry from door to door, asking if they knew a Miss Bennet with fine eyes and a lovely countenance?

No, he had given up on trying to find the woman he had most grievously wronged, reasoning that even if in the unlikely event that he did find her, she would not be inclined to listen to his apology. Why should she?

It had not stopped him thinking about her. Rather frequently, as it turned out. Every young woman he met thereafter was subjected to a rather unfair comparison to the mysterious, heroic Miss Bennet. He could not imagine anyone else acting with such decisiveness; such wonderful tact and kindness. And she had not expected a thing in return. That was the worst of it.

He had accepted that she was lost to him.

And now here she was, on the other side of a small assembly room in Hertfordshire.

Darcy forgot himself. He was dimly aware of someone announcing their arrival but he was gone before it was finished. He crossed the room to the place where he had seen her and was puzzled to find her gone. He looked around, thankful for the small size of the place. He saw her then, sitting with women who must have been relatives. It was clear from the way they looked at him that they knew what he had done.

Darcy swallowed. He had never been the kind of man who willingly drew unwanted attention on himself, but now he saw no other way to express his most heartfelt regret. He took a breath and went to her side.

An older man with wild hair stood in his way before he could reach her. "I believe you have insulted my daughter quite enough," the man said.

Darcy sighed. "It was all a misunderstanding, I'm afraid."

"Even so."

He was about to lose heart when she stood and approached, standing in line with her father. "Papa, it is unnecessary. I do not need you to speak on my behalf."

All the other people in the room had turned quite unsubtly to see what was going on. It was a credit to Miss Bennet and her father that they kept their voices low. It was obvious that neither wished to cause a scene or to embarrass Darcy. This only made him feel worse. How could he have believed her wicked enough to work with Wickham?

"May I speak to you?" He looked around at all the faces that were watching them.

"I hardly think that's a good idea. Do you?"

"It is important. When we met last year, I..."

"Mr. Darcy," she said, her voice even and her expression neutral. "I cannot think of a thing you could have to say to me. You have insulted me enough as it is."

"But Miss Bennet, please. I—"

"You have said all you need to say. All I ask now is that you leave me in peace."

She was quite resolved on the matter, he could see.

27

"Lizzy, what were you thinking?" Charlotte Lucas hissed a few minutes later when they had moved to a quiet corner at Charlotte's insistence. "I saw how he looked at you. Perhaps he wanted to ask you to dance."

Elizabeth had not told her friend the whole story about her encounter with Mr. Darcy. Oh, it was not out of any respect for the odious gentleman; rather it was because of her great fondness for his sister. She did not wish to spread the tale of that young woman's near-demise.

"Charlotte, do you remember I told you about a gentleman whose conduct shocked me? The man who verbally abused me in Ramsgate?"

Charlotte gasped so loudly that a pair of old women who were sitting close by turned to look at them and see what was the matter. "No. It cannot be! He is a friend of Mr. Bingley!"

Elizabeth nodded. "Yes. That is the problem, you see. Mr. Bingley is our neighbour now, though I daresay it makes me very curious about his character if he associates with a man like that."

"He is wealthy—that much is clear from his clothing."

Elizabeth shook her head. Charlotte had always been the more practical of the two. "I know what you are thinking. Believe me; if you had been there you would share my opinion. He is an awful man."

"I have never understood it," Charlotte whispered. "Who could speak to you so unkindly? I had fancied it was a drunken vagrant but it is clear that Mr. Darcy is a gentleman. Why would he speak to you in such a way?"

Elizabeth shook her head, reasoning that silence was the most subtle way of carrying on. "It does not matter to me," she said. "As far as I am concerned, Mr. Darcy may as well be invisible. I shall not allow myself to waste a single thought on him."

⁂

ELIZABETH'S UNEASINESS returned when she saw

that Jane was dancing with Mr. Bingley again. That in itself was no great surprise. After all, these assemblies were usually small affairs, and the usual rules of society were often eschewed if it meant the dancing could continue. No, it was the looks on their faces that caused her so much concern.

She had never seen Jane look so happy. It was true, Jane was a good-humoured girl who always had a smile on her face but this was different. Elizabeth could tell without even having to consult her sister that she was falling in love with Mr. Bingley even as they danced those first dances together.

The little she had seen of him suggested that he was a kind, cordial man. But that was completely at odds with the company he kept. For how could a nice young man associate with the kind of suspicious, prideful man that Darcy had revealed himself to be?

She sat watching them, wondering how she might broach the topic with her sister. This was certainly not the place to do so.

Darcy had surprised her by speaking to her so openly and risking his reputation. She had thought him far more restrained than that. Then again, she supposed, he probably did not care much for the people of Meryton

Oh, stop thinking about him, will you? she told herself. *He is not worth your thoughts.*

She did wonder if his sister was in attendance with them at Netherfield. It would have given her great pleasure to see that young lady again. She was not present that evening. She shook her head as she imagined Darcy forbidding his sister from attending such an event.

The poor girl! she thought. *She probably does not get a moment of pleasure. Why I suppose he has even banned her from playing music because it is a pastime enjoyed by lesser folks.*

"You look amused."

Elizabeth started. She had been so lost in her thoughts that she had become entirely unaware of her surroundings. She was staring up into the serious dark eyes of Fitzwilliam Darcy. She grimaced.

"Mr. Darcy," she murmured, careful to keep her voice down and not give people more to talk about around Meryton the next day. "It is rather ungentlemanly of you to persist in following me like this. I have already made my feelings clear."

"Please," he muttered. "Join me for the next dance. I noticed there are not enough young gentlemen for all the ladies present."

"No, I can see there is a large shortage of decent young men to dance with. I shall have to wait until one becomes disengaged from the group."

He coloured.

"Was there anything else, Mr. Darcy?"

"Very well, Miss Bennet."

28

___

"He asked you to dance?" Jane whispered when they had returned home to Longbourn and retired upstairs to their bedroom. "That doesn't seem so bad of him. Perhaps he has changed."

Elizabeth scoffed. "Just because he asked me to dance? Are you forgetting the way he spoke to me in Ramsgate? He all but accused me of being a criminal. Why should I wish to dance with him?"

"You have said yourself that he was probably out of his mind with worry that day and acted uncharacteristically."

"That does not excuse his behaviour. He acted abominably."

"So you've said. Well," Jane said, leaning closer. Both girls were perched on either side of the bed brushing their hair. Elizabeth put her brush down. "What if I told you he had ten thousand a year?"

"I would say that it is very unfair indeed that a brute like that should have so much money when others struggle so frightfully."

"Really?" Jane laughed. "That is what you would say if he asked for your hand?"

Elizabeth threw her head back and laughed, gasping for breath when she found she could not stop. "Really, Jane. That is the most ludicrous thing I have heard this year. No, perhaps in my lifetime. Now, tell me about your Mr. Bingley." Her expression grew serious. "What is he like? I must say, I am concerned that he chooses to associate himself with a man like Mr. Darcy."

THE ATMOSPHERE in Longbourn House became even tenser in the days that followed as Mrs. Bennet hurried about doing everything she could to hasten her daughter's engagement to Mr. Bingley.

One day, Jane was invited to dine at Netherfield and Elizabeth was horrified when their mother insisted she go on horseback and not in the carriage. Her concern was justified when word came back that Jane had taken ill after being caught in the rain.

Elizabeth was thrown into turmoil. She had no desire whatsoever to be in the presence of Mr. Darcy, yet she yearned to hurry to her sister's side and tend to her. Filial love won out over her dislike of Mr. Darcy in the end and she set off on foot, not caring that by the time she had gone three miles through the muddy fields, she was caked in mud up to her petticoat.

And it was a good thing she did not much care. She had not paid much attention to Bingley's sisters before then, being, as she was, focussed on avoiding the awful Mr. Darcy. Now she could not fail to notice the amused looks they gave her when they saw her filthy clothing.

She could not fail to see, either, the earnest look on Mr. Darcy's face when her entrance was announced. She took her leave of them soon after, eager both to see her sister and to escape present company.

She completely forgot about the latter as soon as she stepped into her sister's room. Jane was quite consumed by the cold and Elizabeth could not help but fret. She sat by her sister's bedside and concentrated all her attentions on making Jane as comfortable as possible.

Hours later, weary and stiff, she took her leave when Jane was sleeping fitfully. Her intention was to take a quick walk in the grounds to stretch her legs before returning to Jane's side once again.

On opening the door, however, she saw to her dismay that Mr. Darcy was leaning against the wall opposite.

"Mr. Darcy," she said as neutrally as possible. She did not wish to offend their host by being impolite to his friend. It was becoming clear to Elizabeth that Charles Bingley was nothing at all like his friend Fitzwilliam Darcy. She was thankful too, for it appeared that Jane was very fond of him indeed.

"Miss Bennet," he hissed. "Or rather, Miss Elizabeth, as I have learned you should be addressed."

She frowned. She would not have expected such earnestness from him. "Yes, indeed. You met my elder sister briefly in Ramsgate, I believe." She made no further mention of that dreadful meeting along the seafront, what was the sense in it? She would not allow herself to speak freely in case her behaviour was witnessed by Mr. Bingley and it somehow tempered his good opinion of Jane. It was most unlikely, she knew, but she did not dare risk ruining her sweet sister's happiness.

Ah," he said, looking away. "Is that right?"

"Yes." She bustled past him. "It is kind of you to check on my sister's condition, however you must excuse me. I intend to take a brief walk before returning to care for her."

"A walk? Well then let me join you."

She turned and looked up at him aghast. Why was he doing everything in his power to try and force her to spend time with him? "I do not think that is a good idea, Mr. Darcy. Heaven knows our last conversations were hardly pleasant. For either of us, I imagine."

"Miss Elizabeth," he muttered. "That is exactly the point I wish to address. If you will allow me. Please?"

She looked up into his dark brown eyes. Yes, there was definitely an earnestness in them that she had not seen before. He appeared genuinely eager to speak with her. It was true, also, that the passing of more than a year had greatly blunted the anger and indignation she felt towards him.

"I suppose... I..." she looked around. "I do not know what you can have to say that is of relevance.

It seems to me you have made your feelings on the matter quite plain."

"On the contrary," he exclaimed, looking more animated than she had ever seen him. "My true feelings on the matter have not been spoken and they have been known to me for some time. Over a year in fact!"

"Very well," Elizabeth said with a sigh. Part of her was curious to hear what could have caused such a passionate response in the man.

"Thank you, Miss Elizabeth. I am aware it must be difficult for you after… well…"

They moved along the corridor, silent apart from Mr. Darcy's occasional and stilted attempts to explain.

Elizabeth was still very much in the dark about the important matter he wished to speak to her about when they met Miss Caroline Bingley in the hallway.

"Ah, there you are, Mr. Darcy! I have been looking everywhere for you!" She glanced at Elizabeth and her nostrils flared ever so slightly. "Come along. You must leave Miss Elizabeth to look after her sister. We have devised the most wonderful game: you must come and see."

Elizabeth was left alone in the great hallway watching the retreating pair. She was curious as to what Darcy had wished to speak to her about. There was something else too—a strange unsettled feeling in the pit of her belly, but she could not place it. She reasoned that she had eaten too much of the soup the maid had brought to Jane's room for her.

She thought no more of it as she hurried out the door.

29

"Mr. Darcy is really not so bad," Jane said hesitantly as they walked to Meryton some days later.

Elizabeth started. She had the uncanny feeling that her sister had somehow read her thoughts. She did not acknowledge that fact, however, because she was rather uncomfortable that she was having such thoughts in the first place.

She changed the subject instead. "How can you still be thinking of Mr. Darcy?" she whispered. "After everything that has gone on in the meantime?"

Jane turned and glanced subtly behind them. "That is true," she mused.

They had been joined on this occasion by a new arrival to their household, a Mr. Collins. He was a cousin of their father and, they had learned, the distant relative on whom the Longbourn estate was entailed. Their mother had thus been making a great fuss over him, though their father's reaction was rather more lukewarm. None of the sisters quite knew what to make of the man.

"I wonder how long he intends to stay," she whispered. "And why exactly he has come here."

"Hush, Lizzy," Jane urged. "He might hear you."

They walked on in silence until they reached Meryton. Lydia and Kitty had taken it upon themselves to walk to town almost every day now. Everyone knew it was because of the militia regiment that had recently been stationed there.

Their intentions were confirmed as they entered the outskirts of the town and Lydia became quite overexcited.

"Look! It is Mr. Denny! Over there!"

His attention was caught and the party hurried on to meet him, with many hushed remarks made about the rather dashing young man who accompanied him.

"This is Mr. Wickham," Denny said, before introducing the Bennet sisters in turn.

Fortunately the man's attention was on something else the moment Denny uttered his name. Because Elizabeth recognised it immediately as the name of the man who had very nearly tricked Georgiana Darcy into marrying him. She turned away. Her heart raced as she tried to gain control of her thoughts.

It is probably not him, she thought. *It is too much of a coincidence. Indeed, it is possible that Wickham is a popular name in other parts of the country and…*

"I am pleased to meet you all," the man said. "Who knew there were so many lovely young ladies in these parts?"

And in that moment she knew. This was the same man she had overheard in the inn that night; a wicked man bent on acquiring a fortune regardless of the cost to those around him.

"What brings you to Hertfordshire, Mr. Wickham?" Elizabeth asked as brightly as she could.

"Doing my bit for the country, I suppose."

She nodded. Thankfully with so many of them, she was not forced to make conversation for much longer. After a few moments, the gentlemen took their leave and the ladies continued on into the town.

ELIZABETH ESCAPED from the rest of the party just as soon as they had entered the gate of Longbourn House. Her mind had been in turmoil ever since their meeting with Wickham and she desperately needed some time alone to reflect on it.

What bothered her most was her sense of disappointment in Mr. Darcy. After all, what had she expected from him?

She walked as fast as she could, even breaking into a run without realising it. All she could see when she closed her eyes was the earnestness of his face as he begged her to speak to him in the hallway at Netherfield.

Why did her traitorous keep returning to him? After all, he had gravely insulted her. What had changed? All he had done was make some noise about wishing to speak to her. And it appeared he had knowingly sent Wickham to Hertfordshire.

"He is a cruel man and I am a fool for even considering his request to speak to me," she hissed through her teeth as she hurried along, paying no heed to where she was going.

She was well on her way back to Meryton, as it happened, by the time she began to feel tired from her rapid pace. She slowed down and leant against a tree. It frustrated her greatly that she was nowhere closer to knowing what to do.

Because what was she to do? Alert every young lady in the town to what she knew? If she did not do so and one of them fell for his charms… well, she would not be able to live with the guilt of it!

But what was she to do? She could hardly go around saying that she had rescued Miss Darcy from the marriage, especially when it was clear that Miss Darcy was acquainted with Mr. Bingley's sisters. They would surely tell the tale far and wide if they heard it. And no doubt they would hear it if it was widely known around Meryton while they stayed at Netherfield.

"It is an impossible conundrum!" Elizabeth cried into the still, empty air around her.

At least, she thought it was empty. This area of the path to Meryton was surrounded on both sides by forest. She saw now that there was a figure leaning against a tree up ahead. Her heart started to flutter: she felt foolish for having been caught speaking to herself. She walked on, telling herself that he was too far away to have heard her.

"Perhaps I can help you in that case, Miss Elizabeth."

He spoke just as she got close enough to see that it was Mr. Darcy.

"What are you doing, loitering here? I thought you might be a highwayman."

He shook his head. "I was out walking. I stopped to rest. What is this conundrum you are puzzling over?"

She gritted her teeth. The man was infuriating! Did he have any idea that the turmoil in her mind was all down to him?

"May I join you? I feel much restored."

She shrugged, not trusting herself to speak she was so maddened by her circumstances.

"Thank you. Most gracious of you."

She walked as fast as she could but he seemed to have no problem matching her pace.

"Miss Elizabeth," he said at last. "I must speak to you about the events of last year. It is imperative."

"To whom?" she snapped. "To you?"

"Well, yes." He looked confused but seemed to have decided to soldier on. "You see, I was mistaken. I only discovered that after you had departed. I was so concerned for my sister that I failed to see the truth. I believed you were part of the group that wished to corrupt her when in fact you made a valiant effort to save her from them."

Elizabeth swallowed. "She is a fine young woman. I wished to help her for that reason and that reason only. Despite what you may think."

"I do not doubt it for a moment."

She couldn't help but laugh at this, such was the height of her incredulity. "Truly? Well then my memory must be faulty. You see, I remember you were rather hostile indeed. You accused me of attempting to extort you."

He looked pained by this. "Yes. Well. You see I thought you were in league with them."

"In league with them? Whatever gave you that idea?"

"It was…" he stopped and looked at her. "I had ridden all the way there from Derbyshire overnight. I was tired and anxious to ensure my sister was safe. If I acted rashly it was because I was not thinking straight. You must forgive me. You cannot know how many times I have thought of you since that time and wished I could apologise to you in person."

She looked away, not knowing what to say. It seemed like a plausible mistake to have made, particularly in a tired state.

"I must thank you again, Miss Bennet... Miss Elizabeth. I... you cannot know how much I admire you."

She baulked at this. "Admire me? You do not know me. Last time we spoke you believed I was little more than a common fraud."

"Yes, well... it is true, despite what you may believe. In fact I do not understand how it has come to be, but I care for you a great deal."

Elizabeth had heard enough. Mr. Bingley was not within earshot now and even if he had been, she was not sure she would have been able to restrain herself, even for Jane's sake. "Care for me? Care for me? My goodness, Mr. Darcy. I feel you have failed to grasp the meaning of the word. Why, how can you profess to care for me? Your past behaviour aside, you have put me in the most awkward position.

"Oh yes, I am sure you felt rather proud of yourself when you banished Mr. Wickham to Hertfordshire. And I can see why that was cause for celebration. But please. Do not tell me you care for me when I am now forced to choose between keeping your sister's secret and protecting those young women in Meryton who are unlucky enough to have any sort of fortune to their name."

She sucked in a breath as Darcy stared at her, seemingly bewildered.

"I am afraid I do not know what you mean."

"Of course you do," she whispered, shaking her head. She was disgusted at herself more than anything. For had she not, for the slightest moment, allowed her heart to swell with happiness on hearing that this man cared for her? She was a fool! "You brought Mr. Wickham here as a means of keeping him away from your own distinguished circle."

He went pale and shook his head.

Elizabeth smiled. "Do you deny, Mr. Darcy, that after I left Ramsgate you were successful in finding Mr. Wickham?"

"That is correct, yes. Surely you can understand that."

"Of course, Mr. Darcy," she said. "And I can't help but assume that you came to some sort of arrangement with him. You must have in order to satisfy yourself he would not return to find your sister again."

He was silent for a long moment. Then he nodded. "It was the most prudent approach."

"And by doing so, I expect you maintain a

degree of control over the man—of his actions and movements."

"I hardly think…" he stopped. "He is not a man whose actions are easily controlled. I will admit that I imposed certain conditions and forbade him from venturing to certain parts of the country."

"Of course," she said. "Because he is a dangerous sort who cannot be trusted."

"That is an understatement."

"Why then," she asked, eyes flashing. "Do you profess to care for me when you have sent this snake of a man to live not five miles from my family?"

30

The next several days were most unsatisfying. The rain was so heavy and relentless that the Bennet sisters had no choice but to abandon their usual amusement of venturing into Meryton. Elizabeth was glad of this in a way: it meant that she did not have to address the question of what she ought to do with her knowledge of Mr. Wickham.

The rain frustrated her too: she had never felt so confused in her life and now she was stuck to the confines of the house, unable to walk and examine her thoughts.

"What is the matter, Lizzy?"

"Nothing," she said with a sigh. "It is… Well I shall tell you a part of it. Mr. Wickham, that young man who is to join the militia and whom Lydia cannot stop herself from talking about, is none other than the young man who very nearly ran off with Mr. Darcy's sister."

"Lizzy! My goodness!"

"Yes," Elizabeth said. "And I suspect he would not be here had it not been for Darcy's intervention. The man admitted he paid Wickham to stay away."

"Well I suppose I can understand in a way. After all, he was protecting his sister. He did not know we were here."

"That is Darcy, though, is it not. His family is safe and well and he could not care a jot about other young ladies who might be at risk of Mr. Wickham's attentions."

Jane looked incredulous. "But it is not his job to care," she whispered, taking her sister's hand. "Besides, I do not think any of us are at risk of being the target of his next scheme. None of us has any fortune to speak of thanks to the entail on our father's estate!"

"You are right. It is just…"

"Come on, Lizzy. You must forget about this Darcy fellow. I know it is difficult when he is so close by, but he will not be there forever."

"What if you marry Bingley? Then he will remain in your circle of acquaintance." It was strange. The thought both heartened her and infuriated her. What was Darcy's hold over her?

Jane laughed. "Well that is silly. It is far from settled."

The sight of her sister's smile improved Elizabeth's spirits. "Well it is as close to being settled as it can be, I imagine, without the question itself being put to you. Have you not seen the way he looks at you?"

"Lizzy! Do not! You must not get my hopes up like this when it is altogether possible that I am imagining it and he has no more love for me than he does for Sir William."

"Indeed," Elizabeth murmured, knowing she would get no sense from Jane on the matter.

ELIZABETH HAD DECIDED what she must do on the eve of the ball at Netherfield. It was with a heavy heart that she did so, but she knew it was the right course of action. After all, Lydia and Kitty had been talking non-stop about the dashing Mr. Wickham and how each wanted to be the first to dance with him at the ball.

She could not—would not—allow one of her sisters to be the next victim of his wicked ways.

"I have something to tell you all," she said sharply when the dinner plates had been cleared away.

Everyone fell silent. It was not like Elizabeth to address the table in such a solemn way. If it had been Mary, on the other hand… well, her pronouncements were so common that her sisters barely listened anymore.

"What is it, Lizzy?"

"Papa, it is a rather indelicate matter, but I feel I must address it. We are all out." She sighed. "It is Mr. Wickham, one of the men from the regiment."

"We know him!" Lydia cried. "He is such wonderful fun."

"And a wonderful dancer too, I expect," Kitty added.

"Silence. Let your sister speak."

"I am afraid it does not reflect well on Mr. Wickham. You see, when we were in Ramsgate last year, I learned some very disturbing news about a George Wickham. He has, in the past, been guilty of trying to trick wealthy young women into marrying him!"

There was a chorus of gasps at the table.

"Well," Mr. Bennet said, gesturing to his two younger daughters. "He is welcome to these two."

Mr. Collins pursed his lips in distaste.

"Oh, you need not worry, my good man. You see, they do not have a penny to rub together. They are quite safe!"

"Oh dear," Mrs. Bennet gasped. "Fancy that! A scoundrel in our midst!"

"You have this on good authority, Lizzy?"

She nodded gravely. "Yes. It is true. I have no doubt of it."

Mr. Bennet grew serious. "In that case, I forbid any of you from dancing with this Mr. Wickham or from speaking to him at all. Do you understand?"

The oldest of his daughters nodded readily. The youngest two, however, grumbled and groaned at this restriction.

"Have you two silly things not heard a word your sister said?"

Lydia scowled. "I bet it is some scheme of Lizzy's to keep him for herself."

"It is no such thing," Elizabeth gasped. "Why on earth would I concoct such a tale?"

"Because Wickham likes me best," Lydia said with a pout. "Even though I am the youngest. It is not fair, mama."

"It is quite fair," Mr. Bennet said, before his wife could respond. "In fact, I think it best that you and your sister remain here in the safety of our home for the time being."

Lizzy sighed and did her best to ignore the howls of protest that emitted from her younger sisters. She was certain now that the tale would not take long to spread to Meryton, especially since two of the servants had been present as she told it. She had made sure of it—she could think of no more effective way to warn the other young ladies in the town.

31

There was none of the usual fanfare that occurred in Longbourn House before a ball. If anything, Jane and Elizabeth went to great lengths to play down their excitement for fear of incensing Lydia and Kitty even more. The two youngest girls had spent most of the day in their room after their father had forbidden them from walking to Meryton.

"It is good," Jane said, mistaking her sister's consternation for guilt at being the cause of their sisters' confinement. "They are miserable now, but imagine how unhappy they would be if they were tricked into marrying a man like that?"

Elizabeth nodded. "I suppose. What troubles me is this. Papa was willing to forbid them from leaving the house today and from going to the ball this evening. I do not know how long he can confine them for. They will surely drive him to distraction long before the regiment leaves Meryton."

"Perhaps papa will have a word with the colonel."

"And say what? That his daughter heard a tall tale somewhere? That is no grounds to dismiss the man."

"Well," Jane said, abandoning her mirror for a moment. "What if Mr. Darcy was to tell the colonel."

"That would never happen," she said immediately, though it gave her a sinking feeling to say so aloud.

"Perhaps… perhaps if you explained to him…"

"I don't see how that would be of any use. Do you think Mr. Darcy really cares what happens to any of us? We are nothing in his eyes; not worthy of protection. No, I will just have to think of some way of shielding them. Perhaps in time Lydia will develop feelings for another young man more worthy of her affections. Mr. Denny, perhaps."

"I am afraid," Jane replied. "That she has all but forgotten Mr. Denny since his friend arrived.

But we do not know. Perhaps Mr. Bingley has a friend..."

"Who you might prevail on to show an interest in Lydia after you marry him?"

Jane blushed. "That was not what I was going to say, dear sister. You tease me so!"

"Only because you are so modest as to be completely blind to his admiration! Now, let me fix your hair. We do not want to leave anything to chance this evening, is that not true?"

———

ELIZABETH WAS FAR from her usual spirited self when they entered the ballroom at Netherfield. She had decided on a rather drastic course of action but in her mind it was the only way to protect her sisters. She did not know when her father's patience for being a gaoler might run out. As it was, he had spent the carriage journey from Longbourn lamenting the fact that he had so many daughters who tested his patience at every possible opportunity.

She looked around. To her dismay, her eyes immediately landed on Mr. Darcy, who was in the corner along with Miss Bingley and the Hursts. Mr.

Bingley was already approaching their little party, she saw to her delight.

"Look, Jane," she murmured. "It is clear that Mr. Bingley feels nothing at all for you."

"Hush, Lizzy," her sister said, her cheeks flushing.

Elizabeth's attention was soon distracted by the group of red coats in the centre of the large room. She would delight in Jane's new-found happiness soon, but she had a task to complete first—a very important one.

"Miss Elizabeth."

She looked up to see who was blocking her path, though there was no need for her to do so. She recognised the voice immediately even if it was far less gruff and formal than it had been the first time she had heard it.

"Mr. Darcy," she said, finding herself unable to look the man in the eyes. "You must excuse me."

He appeared to have no intention of moving out of her path. "I must speak to you."

"Please, Mr. Darcy. I have already made it clear that we have nothing to discuss. If you wish to speak to me about my sister and your friend then I shall save you the trouble. You have no need. I have no issue with your friend."

He blinked. "My friend? What friend? No, this matter does not concern anyone but you and me." He cleared his throat. "Forgive my candour, but I have been able to think of little else since the last time we spoke."

Elizabeth looked around, quite bewildered. It was early still, but the room was quickly filling with other guests. She was alarmed by his willingness to speak so… intimately in such a public location.

"Mr. Darcy!" she said, quite confused by the rapid acceleration of her heart when she saw who was standing in her way. "You must excuse me."

"Very well," he muttered, his dark eyes still fixed on her in the most extraordinary way. "You must tell me and I shall never bother you again on the subject. My feelings are not requited, I take it."

She looked around desperately, eager to carry out her plan before the guests became occupied with dancing. "Your feelings, Mr. Darcy? I do not know what your feelings are, so how can I compare them to mine?"

"I have told you—"

She sighed. "I suppose I am cynical in that sense. I am less inclined to believe words when there is other evidence for me to examine. Actions, for example."

"Miss Elizabeth…"

"I must go," she said, alarmed at how quickly the room was filling up when she had not yet attended to her task. She stepped to the side to move past him. "Please excuse me."

"Very well. I shall never bother you again."

32

E lizabeth was in a heightened state of emotion by the time she had wended her way through the now-crowded room and found the men from the regiment. She did not know why her encounter with Darcy had affected her so much, but it bothered her greatly nonetheless. So much so that when Denny saw her and came to greet her, she found she had not once thought about how she might broach the topic she wished to discuss.

This Darcy fellow is having a ruinous effect on me! she thought. *Thank goodness he has sworn not to bother me again.* She could not even convince herself that this was true. She felt a surprising sadness when she recalled the consternation in his eyes.

"Miss Elizabeth? Have you taken a turn?"

She stared at him for a moment. "No, not at all, Mr. Denny. Not at all."

"I take it your carriage has returned for the rest of your party?"

She looked around. Jane was in conversation with Mr. Bingley and one of his sisters. The rest of her family, including Mr. Collins, were over with the Lucases who had arrived shortly after them.

"No. Ah, I see. No, my youngest sisters were unable to make it this evening."

The disappointment on his face told her a lot and she thought it unfortunate that Lydia had lost interest in this young man. It was obvious that he had a far kinder nature than Mr. Wickham.

"That is a shame."

"It is. Perhaps at the next ball," she said brightly. "Now, you must excuse me. I must find Mr. Wickham."

Denny shook his head. "I am afraid you will not find him here, Miss Elizabeth."

"He has not arrived yet?" She was taken aback by this. She had steeled herself for the uncomfortable conversation she felt she alone must have with him. She might have asked her father, but it would not do for him to confront Wickham. After all, she had no idea what the man was capable of: for all she knew, he might challenge her father to a duel. Elizabeth would not put it past a man like Wickham!

"No, and I'm not sure he will either."

"Has he taken ill?"

"He was in high spirits this morning. I do not think so."

"Well then," she said, before pausing and trying to inject a note of disinterest into her voice. After all, she did not want it known around town that she had been desperately looking for Wickham. "Perhaps he had some matter to attend to."

Denny looked around the room. "Between me and you, Miss Elizabeth, I'm not sure we'll see Wickham around these parts again. He told me this morning that he intended to travel here with me this evening. But that was before he received a guest. That gentleman over there—the rather stern-looking chap. He came to the mess and insisted on speaking with Wickham. I have not seen him since."

"How odd."

"I'll say. Wickham is usually the first to leave for a party. And there was no sign of him! I fancy Wickham owes that man money," he said, lowering his voice to a whisper. "It's the only explanation I can think of. Unless you know something else I am not privy to."

Elizabeth was deep in thought by this stage. She shook her head absently. "No," she whispered. "I do not know Wickham well. Or the other gentleman." To herself, she added: *I thought I did, but it now turns out that I was mistaken.*

Mr. Darcy was deep in conversation with Sir William. She found herself watching him, wondering what had occurred between him and Wickham. He turned quite suddenly, catching her eye before she had a chance to look away. She felt a surge of heat as their eyes met, though there was no softening of his expression when he saw her.

"What have I done?" she whispered.

"I beg your pardon?"

"Oh, it is nothing, Mr. Denny. I must go. I shall pass your regards on to my sisters."

He smiled. "I would be much obliged. Thank you."

She hurried across the room, going first to where her family were clustered. Then she thought better of it. She needed to be alone.

33

A ball offered limited opportunities to be by oneself, as Elizabeth Bennet was discovering. She had been to many balls and parties, but never once had she felt such a pressing need to escape. She hurried out the door, going against the tide of late arrivals. All of them were focussed so firmly on the ball that none even seemed to notice her haste, which she welcomed. If she had been asked where she was going, she feared she would not have been able to come up with a satisfactory answer.

Outside, alone in the darkness, she began to relax a little. She wandered off a few yards, staying close to the house but far enough away from the arriving and departing carriages that she was not in their way.

She saw that there was a path through the pristine lawns up ahead and noticed what looked like a fountain a few yards along it. She looked up at the house. It appeared that this side of the building was not overlooked by the ballroom. That settled it for her. She hurried towards the fountain, assured that no one cared in the slightest about a young lady wishing to be alone. They would, no doubt, put it down to her having suffered some slight at the hand of a suitor.

She reached the fountain and sat on its edge after first checking to make sure it was stable. One never knew with old houses, though it looked as if it had been well-maintained by the groundskeeper.

She sighed. It was a clear bright night; surprisingly mild for mid-November. She reached her hand into the still water and forced herself to keep it there despite the cold.

She had made a grievous error of judgement—it least it appeared that way.

The still night air brought her no answer. She could hear the music from the house. She stared up at it and could not help but smile at the thought of Jane being mistress of its vast halls. That thought gave her solace and reminded her of the importance of the night for her sister.

Why am I unhappy? she thought. *I am mourning*

something I never had; something that was not real to start with. He is an awful man. It is simply my mind playing tricks with me. Perhaps if I was to dance with one of the men from the regiment, I might see things differently. A nice young man. That is it! I shall soon see that Mr. Darcy's predominance in my thoughts is down to nothing more than a lack of real suitors.

She stood and hurried back to the merriment, afraid to be alone with her thoughts lest she start to pick holes in her plan.

34

Elizabeth danced with many of the young men from the regiment, though it was not the tonic she had hoped for. All through the evening, her eyes sought Darcy in the crowd, quite against her will. Often he turned and caught her glance, but he never once approached her, not even when she was sitting alone without a partner for the dancing.

She learned from one of the young men of the regiment that Wickham had been seen hurrying through the town towards the post coach, not even stopping to bid his friend farewell when he called out to him. That did not sound like a young man leaving by his own free will.

She tried to reassure herself that it was all her own doing. Had Darcy not, after all, asked her if she wished for him to ignore her forever? She had not hesitated to tell him she wished to hear nothing more from him.

But that was…

That was…

"Miss Elizabeth, is something the matter?" Mr. Collins asked sharply as she forgot where they were in the dance and misstepped onto his foot.

"I am sorry," she whispered.

Her cousin wrinkled his nose. "You are not an accomplished dancer at all, I must say. Even so, I suppose dancing is considered a vice in some parts, though I do not condemn the act myself."

"Indeed."

She was barely aware of his presence—her attention was focussed solely on one man. Even so, she was glad when the dancing ended and she was able to return to her chair and her thoughts.

Her one source of solace was the look on Jane's face. Her sister and Mr. Bingley appeared to have grown even closer than they were seen to be at the assembly in Meryton, if that was even possible. They danced together as often as they could manage and when they were not dancing, Jane was breathlessly telling her sister how wonderful he was.

Elizabeth felt confident that a proposal from Bingley was imminent.

The thought made her squeeze her eyes closed in pain in an attempt to stem the pain that rose up within her.

Had she not recently received a proposal herself? At the time, she had been so incensed that she had not regarded it as such, but on reflection she failed to see how it could have been anything else. She had dismissed Darcy as a man for whom words and declarations came easily. She had learned too late that he was willing to take action as well. She had no doubt now that he had proposed to her.

It certainly explained his reaction to her dismissal. He had not been indifferent, she realised, he had been hurt by her curtness disregard.

But how was she to know at the time! It was an impossible situation.

She looked over at him now, dancing with Miss Bingley. It was clear that that young lady was eager to get in his good graces, though they did not appear to be forthcoming when it came to Caroline Bingley.

What she would give to receive the same declaration from

him as I myself received just the other day! Elizabeth thought wildly.

It did not fill her with comfort. Because what was to stop Darcy proposing to Miss Bingley? He certainly had no tie to Elizabeth herself after the cold way in which she had dismissed him.

"Lizzy!"

She looked up and smiled at the sight of her friend Charlotte Lucas. Charlotte did not smile back as she took the seat next to Elizabeth.

"What is the matter?" she asked, her face full of concern. "You are not yourself."

"Who else would I be?"

Charlotte regarded her. "You cannot pretend to me. I know you well enough to know that something is the matter. Is it your sisters? I would not have thought their absence would have such a sobering effect on you…"

Elizabeth smiled at her friend's assessment. "No, indeed."

"Well then what is it? Jane has been dancing with Mr. Bingley for most of the evening. By rights, you ought to be thrilled. And you too… you have danced with some of the men from the regiment and I have seen you out there with Mr. Collins more often than is proper…"

"I suppose. I had not been paying much attention after the first dances."

"Is it Mr. Collins? You mentioned you found him distasteful, though it is my opinion that a man with a good living and comfortable home should never be dismissed as an option."

At this, Elizabeth closed her eyes and shook her head. "Charlotte, based on what you have just said, I believe you would think me the most foolish woman in England if you were to learn what is troubling me."

With that, she told her increasingly-astonished friend how she had dismissed a gentleman with not just a good living, but one of the finest estates in the country.

She kept her voice as low as she could and urged Charlotte to keep her reactions measured, but in the end she need not have worried. The gentleman in question did not disturb them once throughout the rest of the evening.

35

A s it turned out, Elizabeth was not to remain without a suitor for long. The very next morning, she was sitting with her mother and Kitty in the breakfast parlour when Mr. Collins made a rather strange entrance. He was more purposeful than usual as if he was about to begin an important sermon. Even noticing this, she was not prepared for what followed.

He cleared his throat and addressed her mother with great pomp.

"May I hope, Madam, for your interest with your fair daughter Elizabeth, when I solicit for the honour of a private audience with her in the course of this morning?"

Elizabeth may well have been surprised by this, had she not been lost in her memories of the previous night. How dashing Mr. Darcy had looked compared to all of the other gentlemen in attendance! She wondered how he would react when Bingley and Jane's engagement was settled. Would he simply ignore her as he had said he would? She imagined he was a rather principled man, and that he would feel duty-bound to do so. She certainly could not picture him putting on a pretence for the sake of keeping the peace.

It would be a rather trying time indeed, she thought.

It was only when her mother rose from the table with great purpose that Elizabeth was shaken from her thoughts.

"I am sure she can have no objection! Come, Kitty, I want you upstairs."

She looked numbly from her mother to Mr. Collins, who looked upon her so intently that the veil fell from her eyes, as it were, and she knew exactly what the man wished to discuss.

"Mama," she whispered. "What—"

She was saved from having to respond by the arrival in the room of Mrs. Hill, the housekeeper. Elizabeth had never been so glad to see the woman in all her life.

"Mr. Bingley is here, Ma'am."

It was as if a storm was making its way towards the house.

"Oh my goodness," Mrs. Bennet cried. "Lizzy! Run and fetch your sister! Kitty, you too! Help her get ready. I want her down here within the… Oh my goodness, where is Mr. Bennet?"

For once Elizabeth was grateful to follow her mother's orders. She hurried from the room and dashed upstairs to rouse her sister.

THE MATTER WAS SETTLED within minutes. Mr. Bingley had arrived alone, and it seemed he could scarcely manage to hold up a pretence that he was there to see anyone other than Jane. Mr. Bennet remarked as much as he grumblingly made his way into the drawing room to entertain his guest.

Within the half hour, the other members of the family had grown impatient and fed up of the charade. Each of them knew what was about to happen if they would just allow it. Elizabeth remained with them for long enough to see that Jane was comfortable with the situation.

On seeing her sister's slight incline of the head and the shy smile on her face, Elizabeth, too, got up and hurried from the room on some pretext or other.

Shortly thereafter, there was a loud whoop of joy from the room. They all heard it, of course, because the female members of the household had stayed within a few paces of the door.

"Oh my goodness," Mrs. Bennet squealed, fanning her brow with her hand. "Do you think that is it? Do you?"

Elizabeth shook her head, not wanting to react before the thing was confirmed, but she still had trouble keeping the smile from her face.

They were not forced to wait in suspense for very long.

The door flew open a moment later and it was obvious from one glance at Jane's face what had happened between her and Mr. Bingley. Bingley, for his part, pushed past them, his face flushed and happy-looking. He disappeared into Mr. Bennet's library without uttering a word.

"Well?" Elizabeth asked, staring at her sister and hoping they had not misread the situation.

Jane burst into tears, nodding furiously. "Yes. Yes it is true! You were right, Lizzy. I didn't dare hope that it might come to pass, but it is done. He has asked me to be his wife and I have accepted with all my heart."

They all looked at her. Of course the matter was not yet settled as Bingley had not emerged from Mr. Bennet's room, but Elizabeth could not think of any reason why her father would reject Charles Bingley as a son.

The clock ticked behind them in the otherwise silent hall as they waited anxiously. Finally, the door opened and Mr. Bingley and Mr. Bennet emerged, both of them smiling and happy.

Jane's sisters launched themselves at her then, a great mass of them backing into the drawing room as they laughed and sobbed and cheered. The servants were bemused at first until Mrs. Bennet emerged from the room, red-faced and shrill-sounding. She announced at the top of her voice that there would be a wedding and ordered a bowl of punch to be prepared for the servants.

36

The wedding plans began in earnest. From that morning onwards, it seemed that Bingley spent more time at Longbourn than he did at Netherfield. His sisters often escorted him to dinner, though neither of them ever said much except to each other. Mr. Hurst sometimes joined them, though his presence had not made much of an impact on the residents of Longbourn.

Mr. Darcy, on the other hand, never saw fit to join his party. Mr. Bennet had no knowledge of the man aside from his rather shocking treatment of Elizabeth and so he did not ask after Bingley's absent guest. As far as he was concerned, they were better off without him.

It was not as clear-cut for Elizabeth. She had

taken to watching from an upstairs window whenever the party from Netherfield was due to arrive, always hopeful that he might change his mind.

He never did. And she was quite certain that he would not. He was a man of his principles. Had he not told her what he intended to do? So why did she not believe him?

Elizabeth had quite forgotten Mr. Collin's strange entrance into the breakfast room on the morning of Bingley's proposal to Jane, but she was given reason to recall it on the day before their cousin was due to depart for Kent.

This time the ladies were all in the drawing room, with the exception of Jane. The Rector of Hunsford entered and made his way into the centre of the room. Elizabeth was busy with a particularly difficult needlepoint that needed all of her attention —she had taken to distracting herself in this way since she had lately appeared to have lost all control over her thoughts and feelings.

Mr. Collins cleared his throat.

Mrs. Bennet looked up. Since Jane's engagement was settled she had not gone to such pains to ensure her husband's cousin was comfortable. That was not to say that she was not eager to see him marry one of her girls, but the expediency had diminished somewhat.

Still, her eyes lit up when she saw the look in his eyes. "Mr. Collins…?"

Her unasked question lingered in the air and an understanding seemed to pass between her and Collins. Still Elizabeth did not notice anything amiss: she had succeeded in focussing on something other than Darcy for the first time in several days.

"Girls!" Mrs. Bennet exclaimed, throwing down her sewing as if it had insulted her. "Come. We must go upstairs and go through your things. I wonder if we will not find a gown that can be altered for Jane's marriage. Come!"

On hearing this, Elizabeth stood to accompany her mother.

"Not you, Lizzy," Mrs. Bennet cried, hurrying the others out and closing the door behind them.

Elizabeth turned and looked at Mr. Collins with a growing sense of realisation. How had she not realised what they were plotting?!

"You must excuse me. I should help."

He smiled indulgently. "Your mother rather insisted you stay."

Seeing no other course of action but to get it

over with as soon as possible, she took her seat and picked up her needlework, diverting her attention by marvelling at how clumsy her work had been up to now.

He sighed and began to speak. Elizabeth focussed hard on her stitching, picking out places where she might unpick the thread, secure it and then go over that piece again. It was a level of perfectionism that was uncharacteristic for her, but then again she knew there was no way she would actually revise her work. No, it was more a way of shielding herself from whatever Collins was talking about.

He spoke at length and appeared not one bit less enthusiastic for the fact that she was quite clearly not paying attention. She was aware of the impertinence of her behaviour, but since he appeared entirely oblivious to it she felt no guilt at her lack of attention.

"When we are married."

Her mind forced itself back to the present away from clumsy stitches that would never be remedied. She looked up at him, blinking.

"Pardon me? I must admit I grew distracted by my work." She knew what she had heard but she prayed she somehow misinterpreted his words. Had he been relaying a story he heard from someone else? She certainly hoped so.

One glimpse at his face was enough for her to know that he had not been talking in general terms or about somebody else.

"Come now. I have already told you it is not necessary to feign modesty. When we are married—"

"You are too hasty, sir," she cried. "I have made no answer, if the question was indeed asked. Let me do it without further loss of time. Accept my thanks for the compliment you are paying me, I am very sensible of the honour of your proposals, but it is impossible for me to do otherwise than decline them."

But he would do no such thing! Mr. Collins continued to speak as if she had not interrupted; as if she had voiced no objection to his plans. Now she could not sit in silence, pretending to listen to him while meditating on her needlepoint.

When he noted that he was not discouraged in the slightest, she was forced to object again. And again! In fact, Mr. Collins appeared to be of the opinion that her objections were encouragement in disguise, so deficient was his knowledge of the true workings of the female mind.

In the end, Elizabeth saw no option but to withdraw from the room entirely. There was no other way: he would not listen to reason!

37

She was not surprised to find her mother outside the door. All it took was one look at her daughter's face and Mrs. Bennet knew all that had passed in that room.

"Oh Lizzy! How could you? Please tell me that you have agreed to it."

She shook her head.

"You silly girl. Come." Her expression brightened. "There is still time. We shall go to him and apply for his generous reconsideration of the matter. I am sure he will understand that your hesitation is due to your upbringing rather than any desire on your part to remain a spinster for the rest of your days."

"Mama!"

"Come on, Lizzy! I cannot bear to think what you must have said to him. Goodness me, you always were a headstrong girl. You must not behave in such a way. Ah, Mr. Collins! Lizzy was just telling me how she made a grave error of judgement. Come on, Lizzy. Tell Mr. Collins what you told me."

She could not and would not do such a thing. Without saying another word, Elizabeth hurried from the house, ignoring her mother's plaintive shrieks.

SHE RAN until she was several hundred yards away and even then she fancied she could still hear her mother calling after her, though no doubt Mrs. Bennet had by now been tended to by the housekeeper with a large glass of brandy. She felt a stab of guilt.

After all, her mother was only trying to do the best she could for her girls. And wasn't Mr. Collins as fine a candidate for marriage as any?

Try as she might, though, Elizabeth could not even contemplate the idea of marrying that man. She slowed down and walked along, knowing there was no sense in returning to the house when it was in its current state of upheaval.

"Perhaps," she muttered to herself. "It was wise of me to focus on something other than his words. For what could he have had to say?"

She had fallen under the influence of a terrible affliction in the past few days. Darcy was entirely lost to her, but now she had the added insult of being forced to compare all other gentlemen to him. And how could Mr. Collins compare?

She walked on, reasoning that there was no sense in turning and returning to Longbourn when she could stroll to Meryton. It was, after all, a fine morning, the rain of the previous week having finally left them to enjoy crisp winter mornings.

Something caught her eye up ahead and she squinted to see. It was still early and the sun's low position in the sky meant it shone in her eyes and made it hard for her to see.

It was a man—of that much she could be sure of—and he appeared to be walking with an uncommon purpose to his step. Still, that was nothing unusual in their locale, so she carried on without thinking much more of it.

He was within a hundred yards of her when the

sun moved behind a cloud and she finally saw who it was.

Darcy.

Her heart lifted with joy before being pierced by bitter regret. Even so, she could not help but smile at the sight of him.

There being no reason for him to be walking in that part of the country, she immediately assumed he was searching for his friend.

"I'm afraid Mr. Bingley is not at Longbourn. Perhaps you missed him at Netherfield."

Dark, serious eyes regarded her. "I have not come for Bingley."

She stared up at him as if she had been entranced by him. "If not Bingley, why…" It was a rather direct question but she had not been able to stop herself. He blinked now; it was obvious that her question had made him uncomfortable.

"I am sorry," she said. "I should not have asked such a thing. It is none of my concern. Excuse me." She stepped to the side in order to move past him, but he stepped with her, blocking her path.

She looked up at him, confused.

"Miss Elizabeth…"

She felt his discomfort keenly, but could think of

no way to alleviate it. "Mr. Wickham has gone," she exclaimed. "I suppose you have heard."

He nodded. Far from seeming relieved by her removing the need for him to think of something to say, he seemed even more agitated. "Yes. After our discussion I reflected on the truth of your words. You must believe me. I did not know you were here. Nor was it cruelty or otherwise that caused me to banish him from Pemberley or London. I was not thinking of others, you see, I was thinking as a brother and a guardian."

"I know," she said nodding. "I must apologise. It was wrong of me to suggest that you had any obligation to my sisters or any other young woman in Hertfordshire. You are not a saint; such things cannot be expected of you. I suppose I... I..."

She stopped. It would have been inappropriate to tell him what she was thinking; that the only reason she was angered by her discovery of Wickham in Hertfordshire was that she had mistaken it as proof that Darcy did not really care for her. And she had not been able to cope with the weight of that belief.

She loved him—and she had only come to realise it after he had promised never to bother her again.

"But they can," he said, clearing his throat. "I *do* feel an obligation to your sisters, simply by virtue of my feelings…" He looked remarkably uncomfortable. Then he seemed to gain a semblance of control of his emotions. He looked her in the eyes. "Because of you."

She smiled and shook her head, fearful of allowing herself to believe it. He must be mistaken. Or it was some slip; some misunderstanding. It had to be, she told herself.

"Miss Elizabeth," he said quickly. "You are too generous to trifle with me. I said I would not bother you again, but now I find I cannot do such a thing."

"You cannot," she repeated in a monotone. She stared at him, her heart beating with such intensity that she feared she might pass out at any moment, which was not like her at all.

He turned and paced away. For a moment it seemed he was angry about something but then he turned back to her and she saw the frustration all over his face.

"In vain have I struggled. It will not do. I can no more stay away from you than I can go on without air. You must allow me to tell you how ardently I admire and love you."

"Oh, Mr. Darcy. I do not have the words to

express my sorrow and regret at how I spoke to you. You see, I had—"

"You must not. My behaviour at Ramsgate was despicable. I only truly realised that at the ball at Netherfield. You see, I was surprised and saddened by your rejection of my proposal and—"

At this, she could not help but smile. "After our first meeting? And our second? You spoke to me as if I was a criminal, did you not? And you expected a favourable response?"

He shook his head. "I was foolish—I acknowledge that. I believed my apology was adequate when it was only the beginning of what I needed to do to convince you of the feelings of my heart.

"I realise that, now that I have had time to reflect on what passed between us at Netherfield."

She blinked in a vain attempt to stem the tide of tears that seemed to be collecting behind her eyes at an alarming rate. They were tears of joy and relief: she had already shed a whole sea's worth of tears at the certainty of losing him, so it seemed only right that a similar volume of happy tears should follow.

"When did you speak to Wickham?"

"It took some arranging. It was only settled on the day of the ball."

"But... I don't understand. Everything I said..."

He sighed. "I suppose I felt there was no way I could redeem myself in your eyes. But you must know that I set about addressing the Wickham problem as soon as I found out he was in residence here.

"And perhaps it was for my own selfish reasons. I could not bear the thought of such a man being in close proximity to you, my dearest Elizabeth. You may think my feelings surprisingly strong for the short length of our acquaintance, but you must remember that I have spent more than a year longing to see the woman who saved my sister from such an ignoble future.

"In fact, I surprised myself with the strength of my feelings. It was only after several months had passed that I was forced to acknowledge that I was hopelessly and utterly in love. I thought I would never see you again, having no knowledge of where you lived. So you can imagine my delight when I scanned that assembly room in Meryton and my eyes landed on your lovely face."

She flushed. Never had she felt such joy, and as a result of the words of Mr. Darcy, no less, the man who had caused her such pain in Ramsgate. She could not help but appreciate the delicious irony of it.

"You flatter me, Mr. Darcy."

He grew serious. "Indeed I do not. If anything, I do you a disservice by describing your beauty with such ordinary words. You must forgive me. I do not have the language to do you justice.

"You have delighted me, Miss Elizabeth, with your answer. I was resolved to avoid you, but you cannot understand how difficult that became in practice.

"Yesterday morning, in fact, I set off on this very mission. I had reached the outskirts of Meryton when I came to my senses and told myself to return to Netherfield at once. I did not have the strength of character to stop myself today."

"And I am glad you did not!" she cried. "Now, let us turn and go in the direction of Longbourn. I fear I cannot keep this news to myself for very much longer without going mad."

38

S he had thought it only fair to warn him about the heightened emotional state of those in residence at Longbourn. She took great care to direct Darcy straight to her father's library lest he come into contact with her mother.

Mr. Bennet's face became a mask of fury when he saw who was on the threshold of his room.

Elizabeth looked from her father to her love and felt a jolt of resolve. It would not be an easy conversation, she knew, but what was the sense in seeking easier paths? In that case, she thought with a smile, she ought to have accepted Mr. Collins's ludicrous proposal!

"My dear, I don't know what you look so happy about."

She glanced back at Darcy, reluctant to leave him alone in Longbourn House given the prevailing attitude towards him.

"Mr. Darcy," she murmured. "Perhaps you would do me the kindness of remaining in here while I speak to my father outside?"

He nodded. "Anything you wish, my dear Miss Elizabeth."

Mr. Bennet's expression transformed to one of animated curiosity. He followed his daughter outside. They stood a few feet from the door after first checking that none of the rest of their family was lurking nearby.

"My, what a remarkable change in the fellow."

She nodded. "Indeed. I have come to learn that I was mistaken in my appraisal of him. You see, there was a great misunderstanding in Ramsgate."

"Was there indeed?"

She nodded. "Papa, you must try and forget everything that happened there. He was exhausted and severely strained by what had almost come to pass with his sister."

Mr. Bennet nodded slowly. "So this is the young man whose sister was very nearly tricked by Wickham."

"Yes." She had not told the entire tale to anyone but Jane and her aunt in order to ensure Miss Darcy's privacy was maintained. For all her family had known, Darcy had insulted her for no reason other than rudeness. "So you can see he was not in his right mind when he first encountered me. I will not deny that his conduct was unfavourable, but time has passed and I have forgiven it given the catastrophe that almost came to pass."

"I see."

"I urge you to do the same."

"And why, child, would I wish to do that?"

She looked at him, her eyes beseeching him to understand. "Because…" she whispered. "Because…"

It was so important. Her very future happiness hinged on him giving the marriage his blessing. She realised now how Miss Darcy must have felt when her wicked governess was attempting to entice her to marry Mr. Wickham.

Her father's face broke into a smile. "Oh, Lizzy, my dear. Any fool can see the depth of your feelings. You do not need to explain."

"But, papa. It pains me that you might reject him because of what has gone on in the past."

He regarded her keenly. "No, indeed," he said at last. "I can see from the strength of your argument that you feel very strongly about him indeed. And that, to me, is the best indicator of all. If you have given your consent to the matter, then I cannot think of any objection to it."

Lizzy's joy was interrupted by the sound of a door slamming nearby.

"Lizzy!" her mother cried, her voice getting closer. "Is that you? Come here, girl. I have told your father. You wait until he speaks to you about this."

"Go, Lizzy," Mr. Bennet said, eyes twinkling. "Let me speak to this young man before your mother has an attack of the nerves."

ELIZABETH TRIED to make it to the stairs without being seen, but her mother hastened around the corner before she could get there.

"So it is you! You've seen the error in your ways, I take it?"

She shook her head. "No, mama. May I speak to you a moment?"

Mrs. Bennet looked affronted by this. "You cannot think for a moment that I can be persuaded to change my mind. Oh, Lizzy! All I have ever done is try to do my best for you girls. Time and time again I have seen my efforts ridiculed and mocked…"

"Mama!"

"No, Lizzy. Come. I want you to come with me to Mr. Collins, who has remained here by the grace of God despite your impertinence. You will tell him that you are a foolish girl and you did not under-stand his proposal but you will gladly accept!"

"I cannot, mama," she said, glancing back at the door to the library, which was still closed.

How much longer can they take? she wondered desperately.

"You must! Don't you see? I will disown you if you do not!"

She looked this way and that, casting around in her mind for some excuse she could use to get her mother to go somewhere they could speak freely. Because the drawing room was certainly not such a place.

Mrs. Bennet appeared to take her daughter's silence as acquiescence.

"Come now," she said, dragging her along.

"Mama!"

"I will not hear another word! You have insulted that poor man enough!"

Elizabeth froze. What was an indiscreet conversation in a hallway compared to announcing her news in front of the man who had asked her to marry him that morning—the *other* man who had asked for her hand?

"We must speak to papa," she said, reasoning that Mr. Bennet's interview of Mr. Darcy must soon conclude. Unless... horror gripped her. What if her father intended to question Darcy at length? What if he planned to reject the proposal?

"Well, I suppose he may be prevailed on to talk some sense into you. Yes. Come along."

The library door opened. Elizabeth held her breath. All she could hear was the thump of her heart in her chest.

Her father emerged. Time seemed to slow down as she looked at his face for some clue of what his decision had been.

"There you are, Mr. Bennet. I need you to..." Mrs. Bennet's words dissolved on her tongue as Darcy emerged from the library a moment later. "What... What... What is happening?"

Elizabeth gripped her mother's arm to support her in case she needed it. And Elizabeth believed she might need help when she heard the news. Darcy's face, usually so stern, had told her all she needed to know about the outcome of his interview with her father. She smiled.

39

There was still the matter of informing Mr. Collins, they realised as they clustered in the library. Mrs. Bennet was quite beside herself—with joy, it turned out. Elizabeth need not have worried about her mother's opinion of Darcy. It turned out that ten thousand a year was enough to convince her to give him a second chance.

"Well, I shall have to go," Mr. Bennet said, glancing at his wife.

Mrs. Bennet was now sitting propped in an armchair in the corner of the room, a smile seemingly etched onto her face.

"Thank you, papa."

She smiled at Darcy. "It is settled, then."

He nodded. "Yes, it appears so. I shall write to

Pemberley and send for my sister at once." His expression softened. "She has a new companion now; a woman whose integrity cannot be questioned."

"That is good to hear. I must say I am eager to see your sister again. She is such a darling girl."

He moved away from the desk and took her hand. "She thinks the world of you. And I do not need to wonder why! You saved her from a terrible fate. And not only that, but it appears you had the good grace to explain the situation to her in such a way that her young heart was not shattered from the sorrow."

"I am pleased. It cannot have been an easy thing for a young lady to go through."

"Far better than the alternative."

"Oh yes of course." She shivered. "I cannot help but hope that Wickham does not end up somewhere with an abundance of unmarried young ladies."

He smiled. "I should not imagine so."

"Where did you send him?"

"He will not trouble us again. Before I visited him at Meryton I took the time to speak to some of the proprietors of the establishments he frequented. Thanks to the knowledge I gained, I was able to threaten him with the convict ships if he should ever misbehave again."

"How can you be sure he will behave appropriately when your back is turned again? You cannot keep a close watch on him for the rest of your life."

Darcy sighed. "No, indeed. But given the choice of being shipped to the colonies and taking a position as a steward on my friend's estate in Scotland, Wickham opted to go north. He tried to vanish, of course, but I had a man intercept him as he boarded the post coach on Meryton. He will go north and if he decides to leave, I shall hand him over to those to whom he owes money."

Elizabeth gasped. "It seems a harsh punishment."

"You might not think so if you knew the extent of his transgressions," Darcy said, his eyes darkening. "You were right, my dear. I was too lenient before with the result that Wickham was free to come here. I cannot even imagine the regret I would have felt if he had injured you or one of your family. So it became clear to me that he must be sent somewhere where he is not the same threat. He will have enough money to live comfortably, of course, but he will find that there is not a gambling den close enough that he can spend it. Nor are there any young ladies for miles around in such a remote area of the highlands. It is the best place for him."

"It sounds as if it is."

They fell silent. Mrs. Bennet was still incapacitated, it seemed. Elizabeth did not know what had done it: the shock or the joy of learning that her daughter was to marry a man of such substantial means.

"It is really rather extraordinary," Thomas Bennet reflected later, as he sat in his library with his second daughter. "To think that I will soon have three daughters married when today I have none."

Mr. Darcy had taken his leave of them a short time before so that he could hurry back to Netherfield and share his news with Bingley before the rumour spread through the town via the servants.

Elizabeth frowned. "Three, father? Surely you are mistaken. Jane and I are the only ones engaged, unless..." she gasped. "Lydia has not..."

"No," he said, smiling. "Now that Mr. Wickham has vanished I have restored her permission to go to Meryton, but she has not been foolish enough to undermine that trust yet. No, she is unmarried, though I cannot help but think it would be prudent of me to see to it as soon as possible."

"Well then," Elizabeth said, wondering if she had misheard. "You did say 'three' daughters would soon be married."

"I did, indeed I did." It was clear that he was enjoying this very much.

"You must tell me, papa! It amazes me that my mother has not shared this piece of news. Who is to marry?"

His eyes twinkled. "Why, Mary of course."

"Mary?" The next sister after her was a quiet girl, more interested in her books than in dancing. Elizabeth had never seen her willingly dance with a young man at a ball, let alone engage enough with a fellow for him to be considered a suitor. "I don't understand."

"Of course you don't." He took off his spectacles. "But it is perfect, you see. They are perfect for each other."

"Who is perfect?"

"Mary and Mr. Collins."

"Mr. Collins?"

"Yes! Oh he was rather cross when I told him that you were engaged to another young man. He could not understand why we had allowed him to waste his time ingratiating himself to you. Romancing you, as he put it."

She was in too good a mood to dwell on such a ridiculous statement.

"I can see how a marriage between them might be a harmonious one. They are certainly suited. What I do not understand is his willingness to marry my sister. Earlier this morning he spoke at length about his desire to marry me. I say that with no regret, of course."

"My dear," her father said. "I do not think it matters much to Collins which one of you he is to marry. To him, marriage is something his patroness Lady Catherine has tasked him with. Of course, I still had to approach the matter with a degree of tact. I expressed my deep sorrow at the confusion and explained that my wife had been unaware of the imminent engagement. I said," he chucked and replaced his spectacles, having cleaned them with a handkerchief. "You will like this. I said you were too well-mannered to declare your hand since your engagement to Mr. Darcy had not yet been settled. You will be pleased to know that Mr. Collins has complimented your discretion."

She smiled. "I am simply amazed that he believed it! It is a fabrication."

"Of course it is. But one must at least try in these situations. Still, the idea of asking for Mary's hand was entirely his. Not one minute after I had told him of your engagement, he nodded his head very seriously and looked me in the eye. 'May I be frank, Mr. Bennet. I feel I have made a mistake. In fact it is your third daughter to whom I would be best suited.' Well, can you credit it, Lizzy? It was all I could do to maintain a straight face."

"I have no doubt of it," she said, amused. "But the truth of it is they are very well suited. And Mary is agreeable to the idea?"

"Rather more agreeable than you were," he said wryly. "In fact, she seems delighted. I was rather surprised."

"I expect she will relish the thought of having the freedom to study in peace without Lydia and Kitty teasing her."

"I imagine so. Though I do worry about how she will fare with this Lady Catherine character."

"I am sure she will take to it well. It seems to me that Mary will enjoy having a patron from whom she can learn."

"I certainly think she will fare better in such a

situation than you would. I cannot imagine you sitting quietly as you take instruction." He laughed and his eyes grew watery. "I shall miss you, Lizzy. It will be lonely here with your mother and those two silly girls."

She smiled as widely as she could despite the tears in her eyes. "I shall miss you too, papa. But we must not mourn. We will not be married for weeks yet."

40

M r. Collins departed soon after, promising to return again before the wedding. The prospect of marriage had transformed Mary. She was still a quiet girl but there was a sense of satisfaction about her that her family had not seen before. She had often lectured them about moralities; now she appeared uninterested in doing so. At times she seemed perfectly serene, even when her mother fussed over wedding plans.

Elizabeth and Jane were just as happy. The only blot on their delight was that they would not be able to marry on the same day. Mr. Bingley and the Bennets had already spent considerable time and money planning Jane's marriage to Bingley.

"I am sorry, Lizzy," she said, for what felt to Lizzy like the hundredth time. "If I had known…"

"Please, my dear. How could you have known? As far as I could tell, Darcy intended never to address me again if he could help it. To think that a week later I would be engaged to marry him…" she smiled. "Well, if you *had* known it then it would have called into question everything I think I know about how the world works. Nobody could have predicted it, I think."

"No," Jane said with a smile. "I understand. I feel the same. My own engagement was such a surprise."

Elizabeth laughed. "Surely you do not believe such a thing, my dear? Did we not all say that Bingley was simply mad about you; that we were sure he could propose at any moment?"

"I didn't believe you."

"Well you should have!" She stood and smoothed down her dress. "I must go and make enquiries; see where Darcy has got to. He promised me he would be back in time for your wedding."

"Perhaps he has been delayed."

"But you are getting married in a few days. There is much to be done."

THERE WAS STILL no sign of Darcy the following day and Elizabeth was beginning to worry. He had been gone for most of the week now. He had not expected his visit to London to take so long.

"Has he returned?" she asked Mr. Bingley as he entered the drawing room.

He shook his head, smiling. "No, I am afraid not."

"I do not understand it. I hope something hadn't happened to him... I..."

Bingley crossed the room to where she stood at the mantle. "You must not worry. You have my word. Darcy is in as good health as always. And you know his sister is due to arrive tomorrow. Perhaps he has been detained by buying her some gift. He is a very generous brother."

She paced around the room, reassuring them all that she was not worrying; that she was simply reflecting on some other matter. She knew they were not fooled.

Dinner was called and they had all started to move towards the door when something flew into the room. Elizabeth recoiled before she realised it was Kitty.

"What are you doing, Kitty? You cannot bound

around the place like this! We shall have guests here soon."

"Sorry, mama," Kitty said without a hint of contrition in her shining eyes. "Darcy is coming! I saw him from the window!"

Elizabeth gasped and hurried to the door. It seemed to take an age for his carriage to reach the house and another for him to jump down from it. When he finally got out, she could not stop herself from hurrying over to him.

"My dear! I thought you would never arrive!"

"I have missed you terribly."

"And I you. I worried you would not make it back here in time for Jane's wedding."

He frowned. "Of course I was going to make it back. I would not miss my own wedding."

"Oh I know that. But Jane's is in two days and I worried that you had been delayed in London."

"I was certainly delayed," he said softly, handing her a roll of paper tied with a string of leather.

She took it but did not open it, so distracted was she by his return. "Did you manage to conclude the affairs you had to attend to?"

He smiled and took her free hand, the one that wasn't clinging to the paper. "I believe I did at last.

It was a lot more onerous than I had first thought, but infinitely worth it in my view."

"I see." They must have spent hours walking together in the grounds of Netherfield since she had agreed to marry him, but she could not claim to know the first thing about how he managed his affairs. That had little to do with her, in her view.

"Yes, rather satisfactory indeed. Do you not wish to know what I was doing?"

She shook her head, unable to take her eyes off him. She wondered if she would ever get over the feeling of disbelief that this wonderful man was to be her husband. "That is not my concern."

He seemed hurt. "Oh," he said, frowning. "I was of the opinion that you were very much a party to this matter."

She shook her head laughing. "You are confusing me, Mr. Darcy. Is that your intention?"

"No, my dear," he said softly, lifting her hand to his lips and kissing it. "My intention is to marry you."

"And you shall! In a matter of weeks."

"No," he said.

"No?"

He shook his head. "I'm afraid not."

She was crestfallen and could do nothing to hide it. "What has happened?"

To her great surprise, he started to laugh. When he had gained control again, which did not take long—unsurprisingly, for a man like Darcy—he nodded at the papers in her hand. "For goodness sake, my darling Elizabeth, why haven't you looked yet? I thought you were an inquisitive woman."

"I am," she said, untying the string and unrolling the thick pages as carefully as she could with trembling fingers. "But I do not care about papers. I care only about seeing you again after your absence."

"My dear," he said with such force of feeling that she felt her heart soar. "I suspect you will care a lot about these particular papers."

She pulled them open, impatient to see what was inside. All the while he watched her carefully. She could tell he wanted to see her reaction.

"Well, go on," he urged.

She glanced down. At first she thought it was some legal matter. It looked rather official what with the blood red wax seal at the bottom. She leapt to the assumption that it concerned Wickham; that Darcy had somehow had reason to follow through on his threat to have the man imprisoned.

Then, slowly, she read over the words.

"Oh," she gasped.

"Indeed," Darcy said, dryly. "Now you understand my haste in getting to London."

"I do," she exclaimed, her heart even more filled with love than she had been in those heady days.

She held in her hands a special licence for them to marry, signed by the Archbishop of Canterbury himself!

"Well in that case I had better take care of this. I believe you have muslins to buy. And goodness knows what else."

41

Darcy was teasing her, as it turned out. While in London, he had paid a visit to Gracechurch Street and sought the help of her aunt to purchase the finest muslins, ribbons and finery on his account. He had carried them into the house himself after she had hurried inside, screaming for Jane and her mother to come quickly.

Two days was not a lot of time to plan a marriage, but it did not matter to Elizabeth. After all, she was marrying Darcy. In any case, most of the arrangements had already been made; all of their friends were already on their way to Longbourn to celebrate Jane's marriage.

Bingley's tastes were far more extravagant than Darcy's, which did not surprise anyone who had attended the ball at Netherfield. Not only had he sent for a team of cooks from London, he had invited most of the town of Meryton to attend. Elizabeth and Darcy were quite happy to go along with the arrangements that had already been made.

Miss Darcy was every bit as kind and sweet as Elizabeth remembered. Darcy had not been exaggerating when he had told her of his sister's fondness for her. When her carriage had drawn up, the young lady had jumped out it and hurried across the lawn to Elizabeth. The supposedly retiring young lady had then pulled her astonished new sister into a tight embrace.

She looked like she was about to do so again as the new Mr. and Mrs. Darcy turned to face the congregation and took their first steps as man and wife. Only respect towards her brother, it seemed, could keep Georgiana Darcy's emotions from bubbling to the fore.

"You are my sister!" she cried, embracing Elizabeth as soon as they had all exited the chapel.

"And you are mine! I thought I had all the sisters I could ever need but I am happy to be proven wrong."

They all beamed with happiness, even Mary,

whose only issue with the proceeding was her regret that her future husband had not been there to officiate.

"Just as well," Lydia was heard to utter. "For we might all have died of boredom!"

"Now, now, Lydia," her mother scolded, for Mrs. Bennet had come in search of her youngest daughter directly after meeting Mr. Darcy's cousin, Colonel Fitzwilliam. "You must not say such things."

"But it is true, mama! You would have said the same thing were it not for the fact that you were too busy trying to marry him off to one of us."

"Lydia!" Mrs. Bennet hissed. "What will people think if they heard you say such a thing? Come on, you incorrigible girl. You must come and meet the colonel. He is such a darling man."

It quickly became apparent, however, that Mrs. Bennet's efforts were entirely wasted. She had chosen the wrong daughter to try and force on the colonel. Though a talkative man, Colonel Fitzwilliam was entirely bewildered by Miss Lydia Bennet and the rather garrulous way in which she carried herself.

The same could not be said of her sister Kitty.

They had by chance walked up the aisle of the chapel together when they happened to arrive at the same time. By the time the party reached Netherfield for the post-wedding feast, Richard Fitzwilliam was thoroughly charmed by the young woman, who was lively enough to entertain him but without the obvious reckless streak of her younger sister.

Indeed, as the merry revellers took to the floor to begin a long evening of dancing, the colonel attempted to halt the progress of his cousin so that he might seek his advice on a rather pressing matter.

Darcy looked at his cousin in that way of his and the colonel felt confident that Darcy would help him to see how foolish he was being.

Something flickered in Darcy's eyes. "Can it wait, old chap?"

Colonel Fitzwilliam cleared his throat. "Well yes, I suppose it might. It concerns a young lady."

"Good. I take it she will still be here when I return."

"Return from where, Darcy?"

"From dancing, of course, dear cousin. You must forgive my selfishness, but it troubles me greatly that I have not yet had the pleasure of dancing with my new wife."

"But Darcy!" the cousin exclaimed. "I have never known you to take any pleasure from dancing! Now you seem to almost relish the idea!"

Darcy smiled. "I rather expect it is more to do with the company than with the activity of dancing itself. We shall dance until our feet grow tired and then you may ask me any questions you like concerning my father-in-law and how it was to ask for his daughter's hand in marriage."

"Why," the colonel asked, flushing. "Would I wish to ask you about a thing like that? We are not young ladies—we do not waste our time whispering about such trivialities."

"Perhaps not," Darcy said, turning to go. "But I rather think you shall soon be asking my advice as to how one might go about doing such a thing."

The colonel looked away. "That is not the case, Darcy, though I wish it were possible. In fact, the opposite is true. I need you to talk some sense into me."

This halted Darcy's progress. He turned back to his cousin and clasped his shoulder. "Whatever do you mean? I was merely teasing. I did not wish to offend you."

"You have not offended me. Now go. I will not keep you from your bride any longer."

Darcy frowned at him, but Richard Fitzwilliam would say no more on the matter. He would just have to live with his sorrow, as youngest sons often had to.

42

D arcy's instinct about his cousin's fondness for Kitty Bennet was correct, as it turned out. Of course, the colonel knew it was an impossible union, what with both of them lacking a fortune. He resigned himself to enjoying the remainder of his time at Netherfield. Now that they were married, the Darcys had moved there with the Bingleys and planned to stay until after Mr. Collins's marriage to Mary. The colonel was prevailed on to stay, and he did so happily.

It was a large, lively party. The group soon fell into the custom of taking daily walks with Kitty and Mary Bennet. Lydia would only join them on the occasions the party could be persuaded to linger around Meryton. Elizabeth kept a watchful eye on her sister's behaviour in the town.

"You must not worry, my dear," Darcy murmured on one such occasion, as Elizabeth stood outside one of the shops in Meryton and watched as Lydia danced around inside with one of the men from the regiment.

"How can I not? She is my sister and I have seen how wicked men can be. If it was any other young lady I might not worry, but Lydia? How can one become more irresponsible with age?"

He shook his head. Darcy no more understood Lydia Bennet than he did Welsh. Not that it mattered. "You must not worry. You act as if it is your responsibility and yours alone, but that is not true."

"But it is," she whispered, before laughing and shaking her head. "I do not say so to make you feel sympathy for me. It is a fact. I cannot guarantee that my father will not grow bored of keeping a watchful eye over her and as for my mother…!"

"You forget, my dear Elizabeth, that you are Mrs. Darcy now."

Anger flashed in her eyes. "That does not mean I have forgotten my family. How can you say such a thing?"

"That is not what I meant. I simply wished for you to understand that you are a Darcy. She is my sister now too so you are not alone in your responsibility to care for her."

She threw herself into his embrace, not caring who was watching. "Oh, Darcy. That is so very kind of you. I am sorry to burden you with the problem of my sister."

"You have not. I understood the responsibilities I was assuming when I married you. I would not change it for the world."

This did little to diminish her sense of guilt at burdening him. For who knew what Lydia would do next? Elizabeth groaned as Lydia threw her hands in the air with joy and began to dance with Mr. Denny.

"Do you know, I think Kitty was a good influence on her. All those times when we thought the two of them were as bad as each other! It gives me some consolation that Kitty will return to our sister's side as soon as the colonel departs."

Darcy's face grew serious rather suddenly. It was an expression his wife had not seen for quite some time now, and it surprised her.

"Darcy?"

He shook his head. "That rather interferes with my plans," he muttered to himself.

"What did you say?"

"Nothing. It is nothing. Just a… conundrum I have been faced with. Now, it seems to me that my sister would dearly like your help in choosing a ribbon or whatever it is that she has set out to find. I shall manage this situation quite well."

She looked at him askance.

"Do you doubt me, my dear wife?"

She smiled up at him. "No, Darcy. Not at all, as it happens."

"Well, then. Go. I would tell you that was an order but I suspect saying such a thing would not be good for my own health."

"No it would not," she said, but she went away nonetheless, confident that Darcy would keep her foolish sister out of trouble for the time being.

43

E lizabeth Darcy's first inkling that something was afoot that she was not privy to was when she entered the house at Longbourn one evening a few days after Mary's wedding to Mr. Collins.

The Collinses had already departed to Kent, since the husband worried that his parishioners had been deprived of his presence for long enough as it was. The Darcys, too, would soon go north to Pemberley. Christmas had come and gone, and there was at last a sense that the place was returning to normal after the frenzy of excitement.

Marriage season, Mr. Bennet had called it, though he did so with a satisfied smile on his face. After all, how could a man find fault with having three of his daughters married in such a short space of time?

There was nothing calm or normal about the scene Elizabeth encountered in the drawing room. In fact, she had to stop and look around her to try and make sense of it, and still the cause of the mayhem eluded her.

Lydia lay on the sofa, quite beside herself with emotion. Kitty sat in a high-backed chair on the other side of the room, glowering at her younger sister. Mr. Bennet was nowhere to be seen. Mrs. Bennet was perched at the end of the sofa, patting Lydia's leg in a rather half-hearted looking manner, though her eyes were fixed on Kitty.

And Colonel Fitzwilliam stood by the mantle looking very uncomfortable indeed, and this despite the fact that he had told them all he was going into Meryton to see a man about a horse!

"What has happened?" Elizabeth cried, for even her quick mind could not make sense of what she was seeing. Her mother had always favoured Lydia, so it was strange to see her look upon her youngest daughter with something akin to distaste.

"Oh, Lizzy," Mrs. Bennet muttered before she got to her feet and rushed over to Kitty.

Elizabeth looked to the colonel for some sort of enlightenment, but he refused to meet her gaze.

Thoroughly confused, she hurried out of the room and went to her father's study.

She was not surprised to find him there given the chaos that was happening elsewhere in his house.

"Papa," she said, hurrying inside. "I understand you prefer to stay away from conflict, but I think you should go to the drawing room. It appears there has been some sort of altercation between Kitty and Lydia. I suppose that in itself is not such a surprise, but Colonel Fitzwilliam is present! I cannot think why, because he told us that he was going to—"

She stopped. It was only after saying those words that she realised that there was only one explanation for what she had seen. The look in her father's eyes confirmed it.

"He has asked for her hand in marriage?"

Thomas Bennet nodded. "Can you imagine my surprise? At first I wondered if the whole thing was not a dream; that I might wake up in the morning and find that I still had five unmarried girls under my roof."

She shook her head. "It is most surprising. I have witnessed their mutual fondness, but he has spoken to me on occasion about his situation in life and how it precludes him from marrying for love. I believed he was speaking of his regret that he could never hope to have a life with my sister."

"Yes, he did mention that when I spoke with him."

"You gave him your blessing."

"I did."

Elizabeth was all for marrying for love, but being aware of both their circumstances, she could not help but puzzle over her father's decision.

"Surely that will mean a life of poverty for them, papa? He has no income and she has no great fortune."

"It seems," Mr. Bennet said, perusing the newspaper in front of him even though his daughter could see that it was an old edition. "That he has acquired an estate in Hampshire."

"An estate? One does not simply acquire an estate, it is—" She stopped as a suspicion began to grow in her mind. "Did the colonel inherit his estate from a relation on his mother's side that we were hitherto unaware of?"

Mr. Bennet sighed wearily. "I did not ask, though I do not believe so. The colonel was coy as to the provenance of his newly-found fortune." He looked up at her. "Lizzy, I believe you have arrived at your own conclusion and I have formed a similar one. The truth is I did not ask too many questions as the young man was already rather uncomfortable as it was. He is usually such an affable, talkative fellow that it was rather strange to see him so quiet and tense. Though I must say, I have become rather used to these odd conversations with young men who seek my blessing to marry my daughters."

"Yes," Elizabeth said impatiently. "In any case, what was your conclusion, papa? Pray tell me, how do you think the colonel came into enough money to secure an estate?"

Thomas Bennet cleared his throat. "My dear, I think we can both agree that your husband is an astoundingly generous man."

44

That generosity, it appeared, ran in the family. Later in the evening, when it was generally accepted that Lydia's distraught state was down to the fact that she would soon find herself quite alone at Longbourn with only her parents and neighbours for company, Colonel Fitzwilliam proposed a solution.

He had not yet seen the estate that his agent had found in Hampshire, but he would be happy to have Lydia come and stay with him and his new wife if that was agreeable to her.

As soon as she heard this, Lydia was like a different girl. She leapt from her place as soon as they had finished eating and hurried upstairs to take stock of her things and assess what she would need for the journey.

Elizabeth laughed as they watched her go. "Kitty is not even married yet."

Her husband smiled. She turned to him and reached over to take his hand. She had sent a note to Netherfield as soon she had helped Mrs. Hill to take her mother upstairs to rest and recover her nerves. By the time Darcy, Jane and Bingley had arrived, however, it was almost time for dinner. She had not yet had time to thank her husband for what he had done.

"You are a man of many sides," she murmured, as Bingley began to tell a story that captured the attention of the others and ensured her words would not be overheard.

"I am glad you have finally seen it."

"Oh I saw it a long time ago."

"Love at first sight, as they say," he said, with a wry smile.

She laughed. "I have never wished for love at first sight, my dear husband. I think it is far preferable to have a love that will last for many decades to come."

"It is indeed." He became very serious. "I hope you will like Pemberley."

"Of course I will!" she cried, shocked that he would even doubt it.

"What are you two squabbling over?" Mr. Bennet said, feigning weariness. "It is done now. You have married her, Darcy. You cannot give her back."

"Mr. Bennet! How can you say such a thing? We do not want her back!"

"That is kind of you to say, mama. Though it hurts me to hear it."

"I did not mean it in the way you think! I simply meant that we have finally found husbands for most of our girls, it does not even bear thinking about to imagine what might have happened if…"

"Mama! We have guests! You cannot speak of us in such a way in company."

"She is right. It is unfair to Kitty and the colonel."

"Oh, I know," Mrs. Bennet sighed, looking contrite. "I am in shock—that is the reason for my indiscretion. What will I do, you see? With all of my girls gone, what will occupy my time?"

"My dear wife," her husband muttered. "It is quite remarkable. You have spent the better part of seven or eight years scheming of ways to marry them off."

As her parents squabbled, Elizabeth shot a private smile at her husband. If it wasn't for his generosity, her parents would have been faced with the task of caring for Kitty and Lydia. That they were squabbling over nothing filled her with happiness, for it meant they had few other troubles to occupy their minds.

45

S he ought to have known that something was amiss. Darcy had been silent now for over an hour. As she stared out the window of the carriage and took in the unfamiliar landscape, she wondered if he reverted to silence whenever he found himself close to home.

A moment later, she was struck by a thought that refused to leave her alone once she had considered it.

"My dear Darcy," she whispered, not wishing to disturb her sleeping sister-in-law. "Please tell me you aren't worried about taking me to Pemberley."

He looked at her severely. She had started to get used to those looks, which the colonel had described to her at length, saying they could almost cut an honourable man in two. She thought that a rather accurate description.

"And what if you do not take to the place?" he asked thickly.

"What do you mean? I am sure I shall love it. You have described it to me on many occasions and it is clear to me that you love it. As does Georgiana. Why should I not love it too?"

He did not answer. She could see from the furrow of his brow that it was still causing him consternation.

She sighed. "How far are we from Pemberley?"

"Three miles, roughly."

"At least you will not have to worry much longer."

It touched her that he was concerned, but in her mind there was no need for him to be. She had heard so much about the place that she had a picture of it in her mind's eye. She felt like she knew it already. She did not know which part of it she wished to explore first, though Georgiana had insisted on taking her directly to the music room to show her the beautiful instrument Darcy had bought for her the year before.

Elizabeth closed her eyes and pictured it. Yes, she could see it all as they had described it to her.

The fine rugs and carpets. The paintings commissioned by Darcy's father and grandfather through the years. She had an image of it all, right down to the kennels and the stables and the vast lake she had heard so much about.

When she finally opened her eyes, a strangled cry escaped her lips. Darcy sat forward immediately.

"What is it, my darling?"

Georgiana stirred beside Elizabeth, who shook her head, unable to speak.

The carriage had rounded a corner and she had caught her first sight of Pemberley as she opened her eyes. It was magnificent; quite simply the largest house she had ever seen. The day was sunny despite it being January, and the light bounced off the many windows giving the whole place a sense of otherworldliness.

They were still some distance away, but she could see no boundary wall, no matter how much she squinted.

"When shall we reach it?"

"It is there," he said, agitated. "Can you not see?"

She laughed. "No, I did not mean the house. I mean your estate. Will you tell me when we reach it? I should like to get out and walk the remaining distance. You see, I wish to start from the beginning. Otherwise I do not know how I will explore it all."

"I'm afraid that isn't possible. We—"

"Why ever not, Darcy? It is a reasonable request, is it not? Pray tell, you have never disapproved of my walks before."

"No indeed," he said, somewhat bemused-looking. "I wholeheartedly approve. What I was trying to tell you was I'm afraid you have missed the walls of the estate. We came through them some time back. I thought you must have seen them."

"Very well," she said, rushing forward to his side and banging on the wall of the carriage as hard as she could. When it drew to a stop, she opened the door and leapt out.

"What are you doing?" her husband cried.

She smiled up at him. "I do not wish to be driven through the place. I want to feel the soul of it!"

"You are quite mad," he muttered, though he too jumped to his feet and gladly climbed out to join her.

46

Six months later

"Do you recall, my dear, your haste to run in the grounds when you first arrived here?"

Elizabeth looked up at her husband and smiled. "You thought I was quite mad."

"I did," he agreed.

They fell silent. It was a blissfully warm July day, though the heat was not quite as agreeable to Elizabeth Darcy as she usually found it. That was one of the oddities of being heavily with child: the summer heat was oppressive now where once she had delighted in it.

That was not the only thing that had changed. She had kept up her daily walks for as long as she could, but her ankles had taken to swelling to twice their usual size so walking was no longer comfortable.

"My dear husband. How many times have I assured you that I am perfectly fine with this arrangement?"

He looked sceptical and she had to look away. It was true that she played down her restlessness for fear of worrying him, but she had accepted it as a temporary stricture—nothing more.

"You love to walk. You cannot tell me that you do not miss it."

"I do," she admitted at last. "But it is not the great misfortune that you seem to think it is. I cannot walk without stumbling. I cannot be the only woman to suffer this affliction."

"But it must be maddening! Do you not remember? We used to walk every day before it became difficult for you. You even felt the need to jump out of our carriage so that you could walk to the house when you first arrive! It is in your nature. I hate to think of you being deprived of an activity you love."

She rubbed her swollen belly and shook her head. "Darcy. Will you please listen to me? Yes, it is something of a hindrance. But you are asking me the wrong question entirely."

"What is the correct question? I fear you are speaking in riddles."

She closed her eyes and leaned back in her chair, sipping on the fresh lemonade that Mrs. Reynolds had brought out to them on a silver tray. The summer breeze was picking up and it was deliciously refreshing on her hot skin.

"Well? You know I have the resources to buy you a low, open carriage if you feel that might be a substitute. You can ride it across the lawns—I do not care."

At this, she could not hold back her laughter any longer. Darcy took great pride in his immaculate estate and she could not imagine him putting up with them being ruined by hoof prints and wheel tracks. "My love, you do not understand it! I am perfectly happy! I love you endlessly and our child will soon be born! You see, the question you ought to ask is would I change any of this for the world?"

"Well?" he asked. "Would you?"

"Of course not!" she cried. "I would not change it for anything! I shall walk and walk once our child is born, but for now I am perfectly content. You have my word."

The End

Made in the USA
Middletown, DE
11 October 2017